Kentucky Summers

Coty & The Wolf Pack

KENTUCKY SUMMERS

COTY & THE WOLF PACK

To Karla,
Have Big Adventures.

Blessings,

TIM CALLAHAN

7-21-10

TATE PUBLISHING & Enterprises

Published by Tate Publishing & Enterprises, LLC
127 E. Trade Center Terrace | Mustang, Oklahoma 73064 USA
1.888.361.9473 | www.tatepublishing.com

Tate Publishing is committed to excellence in the publishing industry. The company reflects the philosophy established by the founders, based on Psalm 68:11,
"The Lord gave the word and great was the company of those who published it."

Book design copyright © 2008 by Tate Publishing, LLC. All rights reserved.
Cover design by Kellie Southerland
Interior design by Kandi Evans
Photography by Tim Callahan

Published in the United States of America

ISBN: 978-1-60604-672-2
1. Southern Fiction / Juvenile, Adult
08.12.09

1 GIRLS

It was the last day of school at Roosevelt Elementary. Fifth grade would be over in ten minutes. We had just turned in our books and Mrs. Taylor was giving back papers and tests. Mrs. Taylor kept telling us how much she'd miss us. I doubted it. She always seemed frustrated and upset with our class. Deep down, I thought she'd be glad to get rid of us. I knew I'd be glad to get out of school for the summer. Saturday, I'd be going to Kentucky to spend the summer with my grandparents—again.

Last summer was the most exciting three months of my life, and I was already thinking of fishing and swimming and spending time with my grandparents. I thought about catching crawdads and minnows in the creeks and hiking through the woods listening and watching the birds and animals. Most of all, I thought about Susie, her smile and freckles and the kiss. I gave Susie a heart necklace when I left and she gave me a kiss on the cheek. I had written to her since then, and she wrote back several times. I'm looking forward to seeing her again. Last summer I kept hurting and embarrassing her, I planned on being more careful this summer.

I hadn't heard anything Mrs. Taylor said in the past ten minutes, and the bell was ringing for the last time of my fifth grade school year. My thoughts were on Kentucky, as they were most of the time. I got up to leave and Mrs. Taylor said, "Timmy, I hope you have a great time in Kentucky this summer."

"I will, Mrs. Taylor. Thanks."

"I want you to come tell me about your adventures again this fall," she said as I hurried out of the classroom. As I walked out she added, "Especially if it's half as exciting as last summer." I waved over my shoulder without looking back.

The first day of class last fall we were given an assignment to write an essay about what we did over the summer. I hated writing essays, but at least I had something I could write about. This is what my essay said:

My Summer

I went to Kentucky to spend the summer with my grandparents. My friend Susie got a crawdad caught in her hair when she lifted a rock too fast. She flipped off the crawdad into my mom's tea. I got caught in a cave and then found my way out. I almost drowned. I found Mrs. Robbins's dead body in her house. I trapped the killer of Mrs. Robbins in the same cave that I had been trapped in. He shot at me and the bats scared him. He fell and died. I got a hundred dollars reward money.

The End

Mrs. Taylor awarded me a C for my essay and had me stand and explain my essay in more detail. Every time I would explain something, someone had another question. I had to tell all about the Tattoo Man and how he had threatened me and my grandparents. I had to tell them about following him to his cabin. I told them about leading the police to find the Tattoo Man and how he had broken every window and light in the police cars. It took forever. Usually I got picked on in school by the bullies because of my speech impediment, but this year, they left me alone.

I walked out of the school building and felt so relieved and happy, a smile spread across my face and I began running up the street toward home. I ran around the corner and down another street and turned at the next corner and rushed past all the small Cape Cod-shaped houses to our stucco four-room house that my parents rented. I turned and hurried across our yard and ran up the steps and burst into the front door and dropped on the couch, exhausted.

"Is that you Timmy?" Mom yelled.

"Yes."

"Did they let you out of school early?"

"No. I ran all the way home."

"Timmy, Timmy!" Janie yelled. My three-year-old sister came running into the room and jumped unto me as I lay on the sofa. "You're home."

I pretended to me asleep. "Timmy, Timmy. Play with me."

I started snoring. "Wake up, Timmy. You're not asleep."

"Yes I am."

"No you're not, you're talking."

"I talk in my sleep," I teased.

"No you don't."

I quickly opened my eyes and grabbed Janie and started tickling her. She laughed and laughed until tears were running down her cheeks.

Mom fixed us hamburgers and French fries for supper. This was my last night home, and I was leaving the next morning. Mom and Dad couldn't take me to my grandparents, but my Uncle Kenneth and Aunt Mildred and their daughter Phyllis were going for the weekend. They said that I could go with them.

It was now six-thirty and Dad still wasn't home. We figured he wouldn't be home until late, and drunk when he did get home. Mom said, "I packed all your clothes for your trip. You need to get everything else that you want to take. Don't forget your new fishing rod and reel."

"Okay." I had gotten the rod and reel for Christmas and it still hadn't been used. I ate my hamburger and fries and then went to my room and put everything I was taking at the end of my bed. I got the Bible out of my drawer. The Bible had belonged to Mrs. Robbins and I had bought it at her estate auction last summer. My parents never went to church so I hadn't looked at it much since last summer. I knew that Mamaw would take me to church this summer, and I would need the Bible.

I also got binoculars for Christmas from my grandparents. I wanted to take it and my case knife I got last year for my tenth birthday.

After I gathered everything we watched TV and played some games. Dad came home around ten-thirty and staggered to the chair and lit up a cigarette. We always had to watch his cigarette until he was sound asleep. He would fall asleep and the cigarette ashes would fall on the chair or to the floor. All of our furniture had burn marks on them. Sometimes the cigarette would fall from his fingers, and we would have to pick it up and put it in the ash tray.

This was the only reason I didn't like leaving home for the summer. I worried about whether Mom would always see the cigarettes fall and that maybe the house would burn down. It also was the biggest reason I wanted to go away for the summer. To get away from Dad's drinking and the arguing that came from it. I worried about Janie, but I knew that Mom would take good care of her.

Dad finally was sound asleep and Janie and I went to bed. It was hard to go to sleep. I was so anxious to leave for Kentucky. I prayed for God to watch over my mom and sister. I prayed for my dad, but I didn't know if God heard my prayers.

SATURDAY, JUNE 4

Before I knew it I was waking up, and it was six o'clock. They were picking me up at seven. I jumped out of bed, got dressed and moved all my stuff to the front door and then ate breakfast.

At nine o'clock we crossed over the Ohio River and into Kentucky. Phyllis and I had played cards and then counted the color of passing cars with Aunt Mildred. I hated that game. Each person had to keep track of how many cars passed with the color they picked. Phyllis picked blue. Aunt Mildred picked red. Kenneth refused to play, and I picked purple. I knew I wouldn't have to do too much having picked purple. How many purple cars would I see?

My mind began thinking ahead to my grandparents store and house and lake. I would hear Mildred and Phyllis rack up numbers as I daydreamed. After playing for an hour Mildred finally said, "Timmy, there's a purple car!"

I looked up surprised and said, "One."

Phyllis complained, "Mom! That's not fair. You're supposed to find them on your own."

Phyllis had fifty-two at that time and I guess she was worried about me catching up. So I said, "You're right, I'm back to zero."

"That's okay. You can keep that one, but no more unless you see them on your own."

"Thanks, one again."

I fell asleep and woke up when we pulled unto the gravel road entering Morgan County. We were almost there. I had not been back since last summer. Mom and Dad said we couldn't afford to go for Christmas and apparently we couldn't afford to go any other weekend either. As we passed Susie's farm I looked toward the yard in hopes of seeing her. No luck and the pickup was gone. Maybe they would be at the store.

We soon pulled into the gravel parking lot in front of the store and I saw that Susie wasn't there. I was anxious to see Mamaw and Papaw. I ran into the store as I always did, yelling, "I'm here!"

No one answered. Where was everyone? I checked the bedrooms and then went into the kitchen. I figured they were in the backyard or at the lake. I went through the back door and yelled, "Mamaw! Papaw!"

I heard Mamaw say, "We're over here." It came from the west side of the house. I ran around the corner and everyone yelled, "Surprise!"

There stood Mamaw and Papaw and Robert and Janice Easterling with Tammy. Homer and Ruby Easterling were behind them. Uncle Morton stood next to Papaw. Clayton and Monie and all the kids except Susie were there. My smile had to be a foot wide. My blind Uncle Morton said, "Good to see you again, Timmy."

Someone put their hands over my eyes from behind and said, "Guess who."

I knew instantly who it was and I answered, "Leo." Leo was the yellow Lab. Everyone laughed.

"No. Guess again."

I guessed, "The Tattoo Man."

"Not even close," the girl's voice said.

"If it's not the Tattoo Man, then the only one with such rough hands that I know is Susie." I turned around to see Susie jumping up and down and laughing. She was prettier than last summer if that was possible. Her freckles smiled with her face and her strawberry blonde hair was longer than last year. She seemed so happy to see me. I was thrilled.

We all walked into the backyard and everyone was talking at once. I was trying to tell everyone how good it was to see them, and they were trying to tell me the same. The seven-year-old twins, Delma and Thelma, were trying to insult me, but couldn't above all the noise. It was so great to see everyone again. It felt like I hadn't really been away for nine months. But while I was away it felt like years since I had been there.

Janice said, "Everything has been peaceful since the Tattoo Man is no longer around."

Robert said, "It has actually been kind of boring around the county since you left."

Homer added, "And I hope it stays that way."

I asked Uncle Morton, "How has the fishing been?"

"This spring was real good; not so good lately."

Later I was sitting with Papaw and the men with Leo at my

feet. The women were in the kitchen, talking and cooking, and the girls were sitting in the grass at the back of the yard giggling and laughing. Brenda, Susie's older sister was talking and looking at me, and everyone laughed at whatever she was saying.

"I'm going for a walk to look at the lake," I said. "I've missed it."

"It still looks the same," Uncle Morton joked.

"Thanks, Uncle Morton. I think I'll have a look for my self. I can't trust your eyesight." Uncle Morton laughed.

As I walked out of the yard and started up the gravel lane to the dam, Delma and Thelma left the other girls and ran to catch up with me.

Delma spoke first, as always, "You want to know what we were laughing about?"

"I bet you want to know what everyone was laughing about," Thelma added.

"No. I really don't."

"We were laughing at you," Delma told me, anyway.

"We think you look funnier with your hair longer," Thelma said. I shrugged.

I had a crew cut flattop haircut last summer. This year I had let my hair grow a little longer on top and parted it on the left side and combed it to the right. The sides were still about the same. Mom said she liked it and I guess I liked it also. It really didn't matter to me unless all the girls laughed at me.

"Well, thanks for telling me what you think. I think your look-alike hair style looks good," I complimented them. They had pony-tailed shoulder length blonde hair with bangs cut short giving them lots of forehead.

"Of course it does," Delma said. "It always looks nice."

"It's always perfect. It suits our faces," Thelma bragged. They then turned around and headed back to the other girls. They looked satisfied with their mission to insult me, and to even get a compliment made it all the sweeter to them. The twins were so funny that last summer I had begun to enjoy our banter back and forth. I now imagined them some day working side by side in their own law firm badgering witnesses until the guilty cracked. Maybe, even when they weren't guilty. Jail would be better.

I walked onto the dam and looked down the lake. A light breeze put small ripples on the lake. I stood at the same spot that I had stood last summer with Mamaw and Papaw one full moon night and watched the large hooked bass jump from the lake and into the moon rays. Mamaw had said it was one of the prettiest sights she had ever seen. Suddenly floods of memories filled my mind of last summer.

"Timmy."

I looked around to see Susie standing a few feet away.

"Hi, Susie."

"What did the twins tell you?"

"Nothing important, you know how the twins are."

Susie said, "I know the twins. I'm sure they said something mean to you, to welcome you back."

"They said they thought my hair looked funnier being longer on top."

"I like it. I'm glad you're back for the summer. Did you miss me, I mean did you miss it here." Her face reddened by her mistake.

"All I thought about was coming back for the summer. My teacher would yell at me because I was daydreaming about last summer and about coming back. I missed everything. I worried about my grandparents also. How has everything been for you?"

"Last summer was so exciting that it seemed really boring after you went home. I think the twins even missed you."

"I guess there was no one to make fun of when I left." I then noticed that Susie had on the heart necklace that I had bought her last summer.

"Probably, but they can always find someone," Susie suggested. "I would like to go back into the Indian drawings cave sometime."

"Me too. We'll go swimming soon." We walked a little while side-by-side.

"Have you gone up to Mrs. Robbins farm?" I asked.

"You won't believe the place. You won't recognize it. I go up every once in a while to play with the kids. Randy and Todd are fun." The Tuttles bought the farm at the auction. They have six kids. Randy is thirteen, Todd is twelve, Sadie is ten, Francis is eight, Billy is seven and Trudy is three. They were remodeling the small farmhouse and adding on bedrooms for the children. I was anxious to see the place now that it was done.

"Do you play with Sadie?"

"Sometimes, but not a lot. I don't think she likes me. She never talks to me in school. Actually, she ignores me."

We began walking around the lake. Fishermen greeted me as we walked by.

"Maybe, she's jealous of you."

"Why would she be jealous of me?" Susie asked.

"Because you're so cute, I guess." Susie's face lit up and her smile lit my face.

"Thank you," Susie said. Then she added, "She's awfully pretty though."

"Yes, she is," I agreed. Susie's smile quickly disappeared and was replaced with the biggest frown.

Our leisurely pace around the lake quickened and our conversation came to a halt. I wondered what I had said that made her change so quickly. All I did was agree with her. Why would someone get upset if you agreed with them? Some things, I just didn't understand.

As we walked off the dam I asked, "When do you want to go swimming and see the cave? How about tomorrow afternoon?"

"I don't know, maybe." She turned and ran toward the other girls and I was left to walk to the house alone. I walked around to the front porch and found the men sitting on the porch. I guess they could tell something was troubling me by the look on my face.

Papaw asked, "Where's that smile that you were wearing earlier?"

"Look's like your puppy just died," Robert said.

"I'll never understand girls," I said.

Clayton said, "Come up here and join the crowd. I live with five of them." Clayton is Susie's father and was the only male in his house.

Morton said, "Why do you think I live alone."

"I thought it was because you were so ugly," Papaw teased. Everyone laughed.

"You're treading rocky, jagged ground, Timmy. This is a subject no man has mastered," Homer said.

I told them what had happened and what I had said. I told

them about Susie getting mad that I had agreed with her. They all laughed.

"She didn't want you to agree. I have learned that over the years," Clayton said. The other men rocked in their chairs and nodded in agreement.

"What did she want?" I asked.

Clayton said, "She wanted you to say that Sadie wasn't as cute as she was, or that you hadn't noticed how cute Sadie was, or that you didn't think she was cute at all."

"You were being tested by Susie," Papaw said.

Morton chipped in, "And you failed miserably."

Homer said, "We've all been there, and we'll be there again." Everyone nodded and agreed.

"What should I do now? I don't want Susie to be mad at me all summer. She's my best friend."

Papaw answered, "You have two choices. Wait a couple of days and she'll be ready to forgive you, or you can buy her more jewelry." The men nodded and agreed.

Homer added, "Sometimes giving flowers will work." The men nodded again.

"But then sometimes a couple of days of them not talking to you is a pleasant change," Kenneth added. The men nodded in unison again. We sat in silence for a couple of minutes. The only sound was Leo's stretching and yawning at Papaw's feet.

"Thanks," I said as I got up and went through the front screen door and into the store. Last year Susie would get mad because I physically hurt her. This time I guess I hurt her feelings. As I walked into the kitchen Mamaw said that lunch was ready and asked me to go round up everyone. I went back to the front porch and told the men and then ran around the side of the house and told the girls that lunch was ready.

Delma and Thelma ran up to me and Delma said, "So you like Sadie better than Susie."

Thelma added, "You're so stupid for liking Sadie more."

"Sadie is like a groundhog compared to Susie," Delma said.

"I guess you're nothing but a *groundhog lover*," Thelma rubbed in.

I didn't even waste my breath arguing with them. They turned and walked into the kitchen and I followed them. I thought that maybe I didn't miss the twins after all.

After lunch everyone left to go back home. They all said they were glad to have me back for the summer except for the girls. Susie walked up to me and said she would see me soon.

"Are we still going swimming tomorrow afternoon?" I asked.

"I don't know. I'll let you know tomorrow at church."

"Okay."

Everyone left. Mildred and Kenneth and Phyllis went to stay with Homer and Ruby. I was finally alone with Mamaw and Papaw.

Papaw asked, "I guess you must want to go fishing?"

I thought about it and said, "No. Not right now." I just wanted to spend time with them. I had missed them and wanted to just talk to them and help in the store.

They probably thought I was sick. I always wanted to fish when I first arrived, but not this year.

2   Dead Flowers Work

I woke early and went to the lake to do my chores as if I had been doing them since last summer. Folks came from all around the county to fish in the pay lake that Papaw had built behind the store. Papaw once told me he made more money from the lake than he did from the store. I picked up the garbage left behind the day before by the fishermen. A few fishermen had paid Papaw and were already fishing, and I greeted them as I walked around the lake. It took around twenty minutes or so to walk all the way around and pick up the litter.

When I entered the kitchen Mamaw had breakfast ready for me. She knew I loved BLTs and had fixed me two sandwiches and orange juice. She said Robert and Janice would pick us up for church in around an hour and that I needed to get ready after I ate. I looked forward to seeing if Susie was still mad at me. I wanted to spend the afternoon swimming with her at the Collin's swimming hole up the holler behind the lake.

We also wanted to swim into the cave that I had discovered last year that had Indian drawings on the walls. Susie and I were the only ones that knew about it. I was afraid the government would take the land if they knew about the cave so I kept it to myself and Susie. It was our secret.

I got dressed and combed my hair and took my Bible out

27

of the top nightstand drawer where I had placed it. I remembered the advice I got yesterday from the men on the porch and decided flowers might be a good idea. I walked down the path to the creek that ran in front of the store and looked for flowers growing by the water. I found some yellow type of daisy and some white flowers with small petals. I quickly broke off about six of each and thought they looked pretty together.

I went back to the front porch, laid the flowers on the porch and waited for our ride. Leo opened an eye and looked at me and went back to sleep. He always had to check to see if the person had food as to decide whether he would make an effort to greet them. The morning was beginning to heat up.

I heard a noise and looked to my side and there sat James Ernest. James Ernest was always sneaking up on people and scaring them to death. James Ernest could disappear almost in front on your eyes, and I never figured out how he did it. He was a year older than me, being eleven, and had not spoken a single word since he was four. He would be twelve in September and I wasn't sure what grade he was in. I couldn't figure out how he got through school not talking. I didn't know how he made it through life without talking.

He was rocking in the chair and smiling at me with a big grin that told me he knew something I didn't know.

I decided to start up my one-way conversation with him again.

"Good morning, James Ernest. I didn't see you coming. Are you riding to church with us?" I waited for him to nod yes or no.

"I talk now."

He said this as my rocker was going forward and I nearly

fell out of the chair. I couldn't believe it. I had never heard James Ernest say a word. I had heard him laugh, and laugh a lot. Was I sure he was talking, or had I imagined he said, "I talk now." He must have thought my facial expression was funny and he started laughing at me and he said it again with this amazing way down deep voice, "I talk now."

"I can't believe this. When did you…. I mean, how… why… I can't believe this. Say something else." I stammered all over myself.

"Something else."

He laughed and laughed at his joke and then said, "By the look on your face, I guess no one told you that I started talking again."

"When?"

"Right after you left for the summer."

"Why?" I asked. I had so many questions, and I couldn't get over how deep his voice was. His voice reminded me of someone.

"Remember when you saw me at the bridge and I was crying?"

"Yeah." I did remember it. I had asked him what was wrong and of course he didn't answer, but I knew something was very wrong. I had never seen him cry before. I had gone into the house to tell Mamaw where I was going and then we were going to play in the creek, but when I returned he was nowhere around.

"My mom had just told me that day that the school's teacher Mr. Dumping had called and said that I had to start talking or I couldn't come back to school. I was really upset. I love school, so I decided then and there that I would talk again."

"That's amazing, and you talk all the time now?"

"Yep."

Robert and Janice pulled into the parking lot in front of the store and I went to the front door and yelled for Mamaw. I had so much to talk to James Ernest about. I couldn't wait till we could go fishing and talk. I picked up the flowers and we piled into the car and headed off to Oak Hills Church.

We greeted everyone and I asked, "Why didn't someone tell me James Ernest was talking again?"

Mamaw answered, "Didn't think of it. He's been talking for quite a while now. I didn't realize you didn't know."

Janice asked, "How long you been talking now James Ernest."

"Since school started last year. Had to, I wanted to go to school."

It dawned on me as to who James Ernest sounded like with that deep voice. "Alfalfa! That's who you sound like. I knew you sounded like someone. Alfalfa, from *The Little Rascals*." It always sounded like Alfalfa had a frog in his throat and James Ernest sounded the same way. I thought his voice sounded even deeper than Alfalfa's voice.

Robert said, "He sure does, I think you pegged it, Timmy."

James Ernest didn't say anything and turned his head and stared out the window all the way to church.

Robert was soon pulling into the church gravel parking lot and I followed James Ernest out of the car and looked for Clayton's red truck. I didn't see it, but we were a little early so I waited outside with my flowers behind my back in my right hand and my Bible in my left. I didn't want the other boys to see the flowers.

Daniel Sugarman spotted me and came running over. "Good to see you, Timmy."

"You too, Daniel."

"Let's play again this summer. I enjoyed last year in the creek."

"Sure, any time, just call."

"Okay, see you."

"Okay." As he turned to run into the church Clayton pulled into the lot and parked. The girls jumped out of the bed of the truck and I rushed over to see Susie.

Delma quickly said, "You still here. I was hoping you had gone back to Ohio."

Thelma added, "I was hoping so too. Susie is still mad at you."

"You girls go with Mom," Susie pleaded.

They turned and stomped off and I heard Delma say, "Why does he have to come to this church, Momma."

"Yes. Why?"

"You girls hush up. What other church would he go to?" Monie said.

She was right. Oaks Hills Church was the only church in the area.

As Susie and I walked toward the church with Brenda I said, "These are for you." I handed the flowers to her, and they were the worst looking flowers I had ever seen. From Susie's face I could tell Susie thought the same thing. They had wilted and had draped down over my fingers and become almost nothing. You could still see a few colors of petals. I had to turn them upside down so she could grab them.

Brenda started laughing and laughed all the way into the church. Susie said, "I guess it was a sweet thought."

"I'm sorry about yesterday when you got mad at me." I wasn't sure what I was apologizing about, but it seemed like the right thing to do.

"Okay," she said, as she threw the flowers to the ground as she started up the front stone steps of the church.

Pastor Black was there greeting everyone as they entered, he rubbed my head, smiled and said, "It's good to have you back again, Timmy."

"Thank you, Pastor Black."

As I walked away he said, "I have something special planned for you this year. See me after the service."

Oh no! Not again. Last year James Ernest and I were laughing at two singers, if you could call them that, and I got caught and had to say two memory verses in front of the church one Sunday. It was one of the most frightening moments of my life. I wasn't about going to do it again. Susie sat with her mom and sisters and I sat with Mamaw and James Ernest.

"Don't you dare make me laugh during church today," I said to James Ernest.

I then told him what the pastor said. He snickered and said, "You did good last year."

I gave him a look and he grinned at me. As the singers were making their way up front to sing I told James Ernest, "Since you talk now, maybe you would like to say memory verses in front of the church."

He poked me in the ribs with his elbow.

The whole service I worried about what the pastor wanted me to do. I was sure it was to say memory verses again. I didn't get much out of the service except he had me stand to be recognized by the congregation. He said they were glad to see me back for the summer. Pastor Black then preached on Revelation and how the end was near and how we would hear the trumpet sound and meet Jesus in the air and then go with him to Heaven. He said that it could be today, but only if we had our ticket punched.

Sometimes I thought he preached just to confuse me. What trumpet sound? What ticket needed punching? How were we going to meet Jesus in the air? He said something about Jesus being on a white horse. I could maybe understand a giant eagle, but a flying horse. Why was the end near? The end of what! I guess I had a lot to learn about the Bible.

As soon as the service ended I told Mamaw I would meet her in the parking lot. I grabbed James Ernest by the arm and we headed up to the pulpit area.

"Where are we going?" he asked.

"Out the back door. I don't want to see the pastor."

We walked across the stage and opened the door and out we went. I had never seen anyone use the back door, but it worked. I escaped without having to talk to Pastor Flack Black.

I ran around the church to find Susie. She was talking to some other girls and I waited until she walked away and then I ran up and asked, "Are we going swimming this afternoon?"

"I suppose so, but not until after we have Sunday dinner. I'll have Dad bring me down around two."

Mamaw yelled, "Come on, Timmy!"

"Okay, I'll see you then." I turned and ran to the car. I was happy; Susie must have forgiven me and all because I gave her dead flowers.

On the way home I asked James Ernest, "You want to go fishing with me in the morning?"

"Sure. What time and where?"

"Let's go around seven thirty. We'll beat the heat. We'll fish the back of the lake and then fish the creek later in the week."

James Ernest excitedly stated, "I'll be sitting on the front porch."

Mamaw suggested, "I'll fix both of you a big breakfast before you head out. How does that sound?"

"Good to me," I said.

"Sounds great," James Ernest agreed. Every time he talked I thought of Alfalfa, and I was amazed that he was now talking. How could someone just decide not to talk? To do it for almost seven years was unbelievable. I wondered how many times he almost slipped and said something. What if the Tattoo Man had been attacking his mother, would he have not screamed for help? What if he was being attacked by a lion? Surely he would have yelled for help. I always thought that he had probably lost his ability to talk. I couldn't fathom that a person could just quit talking.

All it took to get him to talk again was to tell him he wouldn't be able to go to school any longer. Most kids would have grinned and said, *Great—no more school!* I now had a new admiration for James Ernest. I always admired the way he would appear and disappear. This though was a different kind of respect. I liked it that he wanted to go to school and learn things. I would have been one of the kids that grinned and said, *Great—no more school!*

We pulled into the parking lot and James Ernest and I slid

out of the car and ran our separate ways. I yelled over my shoulder, "See you in the morning."

"Okay."

I stood at the front door and held the screen door open for Mamaw. I waved and yelled thanks to Robert, Janice, and Tammy.

Papaw was standing behind the white counter in the store. He asked, "How was church?"

I answered, "Preacher Black yelled about Jesus riding a flying white horse and blowing a trumpet."

"I bet that was interesting."

"You would think so. I gave Susie flowers like Homer suggested."

"How did that go?"

"They were dead by the time I handed them to her. I believe she still forgave me. She's coming down to go swimming with me after she eats Sunday dinner."

"I'll be. Even dead flowers work."

"I guess so," I said.

"Will you watch the store after you change clothes?" Papaw asked.

"Sure." I loved to watch the store and wait on grocery customers and fishermen.

Mamaw made fried chicken, mashed potatoes, green beans, and corn bread for Sunday dinner. In the middle of the table were yellow flowers with some small white ones mixed in. They were alive in a water-filled Mason jar. Mamaw saw the flowers and looked at me and said, "That's awfully sweet of you, Timmy."

"Don't look at me. I didn't do it."

She looked at Papaw and smiled, "Well, thank you, Martin. They're real pretty. What do you want?"

Papaw just looked at her and smiled and then lowered his head. "I just thought you might like them. They look nice on the table."

For dessert Mamaw had made her great cherry dumplings, my favorite dessert in the whole world.

It wasn't long before I heard Clayton's voice in the store and I jumped off the couch, turned off the television, and rushed into the store where Clayton and Susie were standing.

"You kids have fun," Clayton said.

I answered, "We're going to the swimming hole for the afternoon. Can we take a pop with us Papaw?"

"Sure."

Susie and I walked to the large red cooler that had a large Royal Crown Cola on the front. I grabbed an RC Cola and Susie said she would like an Orange Crush. We opened them with the opener on the side of the cooler. We placed the cap under the lip and pushed the bottom of the bottle down and watched the cap fall to the bottom of the can that was attached to the opener.

We walked through the living room and kitchen, said hello and goodbye to Mamaw and walked out of the back door toward the lake.

Mamaw swung open the back screen door and yelled, "Be careful." We waved and continued to the Collins' swimming hole. There were fifteen fishermen around the lake today. I could see that all were fishing for catfish. The weather was nice. Not so hot that the fishermen left in the afternoon heat to return in the evening to continue their fishing.

Susie and I small-talked while we walked and I pointed out the fishermen that I knew. She knew a few that I didn't. When we got near the back of the lake Susie said, "There is where we first saw the Tattoo Man last year. He was leaning against that tree. You remember?"

"How could I ever forget? We were on our way to the swimming hole then, also."

"He was really scary."

"Yeah. You should have been stranded in a cave with him trying to kill you."

"I still can hardly believe what happened last summer. I hope nothing like it happens this year."

"I'd have to agree." I didn't know of anything I could agree with more.

3 THE MOST RUDEST

The water felt so good as we splashed and swam around in the clear mountain-fed pool. The sun's rays were still shining on the water warming it. Because of the cliff that rose on the west side of the pool, the sun would only shine on the pool for a couple more hours.

"Let's swim into the cave and look around," Susie said.

"Okay."

"Ready to go? I'll lead the way this time." Susie was anxious to see the Indian drawings again. Last summer I had taken Susie inside the cave a couple of times. She was the only person I had told about the discovery. I knew I could trust her not to tell anyone else about it.

"Oh man! I forgot my flashlight. It's in the nightstand in my room."

"You mean in Ohio?"

"No, my bedroom at the store." In my excitement I had forgotten to bring it. "It's okay. Once we're inside our eyes will adjust to the dark in a few minutes. We'll have some light from the water. Let's go."

"Follow me," Susie said excitedly.

Susie dove under the water and headed under the rock overhang and into the tunnel that led inside to the small cave.

39

I followed closely behind. I had sat in class as Mrs. Taylor was teaching and I would daydream of the day that I would get to swim back inside the cave and look at the Indian drawings. I was shocked last year when I found it after getting trapped in the bigger cave adjacent to it. I had found a tunnel that was my only escape, slipped into it and slid down the tunnel into the cave that I now was swimming into.

A few seconds later I popped up next to Susie inside the cave. We swam over to the edge and stood up. I walked over to the rocks that formed benches on both sides of the pool. The other side faced the cave walls that were full of drawings of animals, Indians, birds and even a drawing of the cave. Susie and I sat next to each other in silence, waiting for our eyes to adjust to the dim light from the water so we could see the walls.

"It's dark," Susie finally said.

"We'll be able to see soon. I can't believe we're here again. You haven't told anyone about it, have you?"

"Of course I haven't. I keep my promises."

"I know you do. I've wanted to tell everyone, but I knew I couldn't," I said.

"Me too. But it's nice that we have a secret together."

After I had found the cave I had to tell someone about it. It had to be someone that I could trust. I thought I could trust Susie. Now I knew I could.

"My eyes are adjusting. I can see some of the drawings now," Susie said.

I looked up at the wall and I saw a drawing of a large buffalo with a half moon above it. "There's the buffalo."

"That's the first thing I saw," Susie said.

We stayed in the cave for at least an hour studying all the

drawings more closely than we had last year. Our eyes adjusted to where it seem liked someone had turned on a ceiling light. We each decided which drawing was our favorite. I chose the drawing of the Indian shooting his bow and arrow at a bear coming at him, front paws in the air. Susie chose a bald eagle flying with a fish in its talons.

We decided to swim back out and warm up in the sunshine. It was cold getting back into the water inside the cave. I led and we dove under the water and through the tunnel, under the rock ledge, and back into the pool. Susie popped up, I splashed her in the face, and she began chasing me. She could still swim faster than me and soon she had caught me. She jumped on my back and dunked me under the water.

We got out and lay on the dry rocks that lined the outside of the pool.

"How was school this past year?" Susie asked.

"Boring, I guess I'm not a very good student. I daydream too much."

"I do that sometimes, also. What do you think about?"

"I mostly thought about last summer. I can't stop thinking about the Tattoo Man and Mrs. Robbins."

"Do you daydream about anything else?" Susie wanted to know.

"You."

"You really think about me? What do you think about?" she asked.

I wasn't sure what to say. I didn't want to say that I thought about the kiss on the cheek she gave me when I gave her the necklace—all the time. I could have told her that I thought about when she touched my hand. I could have told her I always thought about how cute she was and that I liked her hair, freckles, and smile. But instead I said, "I think about the crawdad getting stuck in your hair."

She looked at me with a blank, disappointed stare. I quickly added, "I thought about how much I missed you." I thought maybe that would work.

"Do you have a girlfriend in Ohio?" she asked.

There were a few girls in my class that were cute, but I hardly ever talked to them. They weren't nearly as cute or nice as Susie. Susie was fun to be with and the only girl I knew that I could really talk to.

"No."

She slightly smiled and asked, "You don't?"

"Do you have a boyfriend?" I asked.

She thought about it and put her finger to her chin and answered, "Yes."

"Who is it?" I wanted to know.

She said, "Can't tell you."

She got up and dove back into the pool. I wondered who her boyfriend was and did I know him. I was disappointed. We stayed at the swimming hole for another hour. We splashed each other and dove after things at the bottom of the pool.

When we went back to the store Mamaw was in the kitchen finishing putting batter into pans for a cake she was baking. She asked if we wanted to lick the chocolate batter from the bowl.

"You know the answer to that, Mamaw."

"Yes, I did." She handed Susie and I each a spoon, and we dug into the batter.

Susie said, "I almost never get to lick the batter at home because the twins are always begging for it."

"What's the cake for?" I asked.

"Clayton, Monie, and the twins are coming down later for Sunday evening dessert with us. I thought a chocolate cake would be good. Monie is bringing a pie. I believe Clayton is going to pick up Morton on the way."

I was glad Susie would be staying longer. She went into my bedroom to change back into her clothes. I changed after her, and then we turned on the TV, and played cards until her family arrived.

We heard the twins walking up the front porch steps. Delma said, "I can't wait to see what Timmy did to Susie this time."

"He probably hit her in the face with a rock or something," Thelma guessed.

"I can't stand the thought of her pretty face being smashed," Delma said.

"She could have lost an eye," Thelma added.

"Not having eyes isn't so bad," I heard Uncle Morton tell them, as the front door opened.

Monie couldn't stand it, "You two girls hush up, and Morton, you certainly aren't helping things one bit. Nothing happened to Susie, I hope."

"Just trying to keep things positive," Uncle Morton exclaimed. Everyone walked through the store and living room and into the kitchen. I hadn't noticed, but Susie had grabbed a washcloth and had it held up covering her left eye. Susie cried out, "Oh Momma, my eye!" She jumped up and turned toward them and ran to her mom. Mamaw and I cracked up laughing, and the twins looked confused. Monie just shook her head.

Susie took the washcloth away from her eye and said to the

twins, "I'm sorry to disappoint you two, but nothing bad happened, and I still have full use of both eyes."

Delma paused for a second while looking at Susie and then Thelma, smiled and said, "I guess miracles are still possible."

"Yes, I suppose they do. This is a perfect example," Thelma added.

"I think the proof that miracles still exist is that you two are still among the living," I said.

"You are still as rude as ever."

"Ruder," Thelma seconded.

They turned to go into the living room.

"The rudest," Delma added.

"The most rudest."

"You are right, that's it, the most rudest."

Mamaw finished putting the frosting on the cake as Monie sat two pies on the table. One was a banana cream, and the other was strawberry rhubarb. It was cooling off outside, and everyone went to the backyard with their dessert and sat in the lawn chairs that Papaw had put out. Clayton fixed a sampler plate with a small piece of all three. He said that he couldn't decide between the three, so he took all of them.

I decided to have a slice of chocolate cake and a piece of banana cream pie. I passed on the other pie. I passed on anything that had rhubarb in it. Susie got a slice of cake as did the twins. The twins got to lick the frosting bowl. They had frosting all over their chins and cheeks. No one said anything to them about it. We just looked at them and chuckled. They got up and went back into the kitchen as they complained about rudeness again.

We spent the evening reminiscing and the time flew by. As everyone left, I told Susie that I would see her again, soon. She agreed.

4 PURTY

MONDAY, JUNE 6

The next morning I walked out onto the front porch and James Ernest was waiting in one of the rocking chairs. He had a spinning reel and a bait bucket. He had gone to the creek the evening before and caught some crawdads. We walked into the kitchen and Mamaw was cooking pancakes and bacon.

I poured both of us a glass of orange juice and we each ate three pancakes and four slices of bacon. After we ate, James Ernest thanked Mamaw for breakfast. He said, "That was the best breakfast I've ever had."

I wasn't sure if James Ernest was just being nice or if he meant it. We walked to the back of the lake and took our places on the slanted rock in the back bay of the lake. There were no other fishermen at the lake. Mondays were usually very slow since most of the fishermen had to work. I would do my chores after James Ernest and I were done fishing.

"It feels real strange talking to you now that you talk back."

"It feels strange to me to talk back. Sometimes I have to remember that I now talk. It had been a long time since I talked."

"Did you ever almost slip and say something?"

"Yeah, all the time. My mom walked into a hornets nest one day. I knew it was there, and I started to warn her."

"You didn't."

"By the time I saw her there, it was already too late. I went to help her. I ran in and started swinging a badminton racket that I picked up off the ground. The hornets decided I was more of a target, and Mom got away with only a few stings."

"Did you get stung?"

"Mom counted ten stings. It would have been worse, except that I can run pretty fast."

"Did you almost ever talk to me?"

"Last year when I saw you at Mrs. Robbins and you had just escaped from the rag bed. I knew that the Tattoo Man stayed at the cabin and I wanted to tell you that I knew." The summer before I had gotten caught inside the Tattoo Man's cabin and had to hide in his smelly rag bed. I escaped and saw James Ernest at Mrs. Robbins house and told him all about it.

"Were you the person who yelled 'Duck Tim' when the Tattoo Man tried to kill me?" I asked. I always thought that it was either James Ernest or God that had warned me just in time.

"No. It wasn't me. I never said one word since I was four."

I was now certain that it was God who had warned me. It sounded like a real voice, but it could have been an inner voice telling me to duck. I sat there on the rock and wondered about this revelation.

James Ernest hooked the first fish. He reeled in a medium-sized bluegill. I hadn't even cast my worm in yet. I was fascinated just talking to James Ernest.

"I really like your deep voice. I can't believe how much you sound like Alfalfa. So, why did you stop talking?"

"Because of that."

"What do you mean?"

"When I was little and talked, everyone always laughed at me because of my deep voice. Everyone started calling me Alfalfa. I hated it. So I just decided to quit talking. It worked. People stopped laughing and stopped calling me Alfalfa."

I remembered yesterday in the car on the way to church when I said he sounded like Alfalfa. James Ernest had turned and stopped talking. I now know why. "I'm sorry about yesterday. I won't call you Alfalfa again. I didn't know. I think your voice is really neat. I would love to have your voice instead of mine."

"Really?" James Ernest said.

"I hate my voice. People are always making fun of the way I talk. I guess we have something in common," I explained.

"I suppose so," James Ernest said while smiling.

James Ernest and I sat in silence for quite a while, fished and watched the clouds roll by. I believe we both were happy that we now had something that bonded us together, even if it was that we both talked funny. More than that, it was nice to have a friend during summer vacation to talk with. I had Susie, but you could just talk to guys differently and act differently around guys. We didn't care if our hair was combed correctly or we got night crawler scum on our shirttails where we wipe our hands off. We could even pick our nose without feeling like we were monsters or idiots.

Two mallards had made the lake their home and had babies. They swam by with the nine little ones trying to keep up. We laughed at the babies bobbing up and down and in all different directions.

All of a sudden a rock landed near the babies and the ducks scattered everywhere. We looked around and standing on the top of the rising of the path was Randy and Todd Tuttle, the two oldest boys of the Tuttle family that moved to Mrs. Robbins' farm.

"Hey, cut it out," I yelled, just as Todd cut loose with his rock. The rock ended up nowhere near the ducks—bad arm.

Thirteen-year-old Randy ran down the incline toward us and said, "They're just stupid ducks. What's the big deal?"

"Would you like it if someone threw rocks at you? Besides that, I like the ducks that live here," I said.

"Well, big whoop," Randy said. "I'll throw at the ducks in our pond then."

"I didn't know there was a pond up there except for that small one for the cows and horses," I said.

Todd said, "Dad had it enlarged and dug it out deeper. It's purty big now."

"Are there any fish in it?" I asked.

"Just a few small ones for now," Todd answered.

"I haven't had a chance to come up and see the new house and all the changes."

James Ernest said, "You won't even recognize the place."

"It sure is different. A lot better than that dump that it was before," Randy laughed.

His comment hit me the wrong way. Mr. and Mrs. Robbins had lived there for a long, long time. It had fallen into disarray after Mr. Robbins died. Mrs. Robbins couldn't keep the place up very well, but it was still their home and she loved it. She even died there. I didn't say anything. They wouldn't understand, anyway.

"You guys want to do something?" Randy asked.

"We are doing something," James Ernest said.

"Well, I mean something with us. We could go hiking, or play ball, or go to the creek and swim."

I looked at James Ernest and asked, "What do you want to do?"

"It's okay with me."

"Okay, let's go hiking," I suggested.

James Ernest and I hadn't kept any of the fish, so we just hid our poles and bait in the woods, and I led them up the stream toward Robert and Janice's house. We walked past the cliffs and around the Collin's swimming hole. Todd said, "This sure is purty."

We walked on around the pool and continued up the trail. Randy began asking me about last summer and the Tattoo Man. I explained that this was the trail that I had led him away from Robert and Janice's to the cave. I went into great detail about it. James Ernest found a stick that he used as a walking stick. Soon, we all were looking for the perfect walking stick. Within a few minutes we all had one. Todd's was from a limb of a sycamore. It was white and gray and as crooked as could be. We teased him about it, but all he said was, "I like it, it's purty."

We made it to Robert's farm. We stood and looked across the field that led to the shed that the Tattoo Man was broken into. I told them about running into the field and yelling at him. We turned and continued following the stream past their farm. I had only been this far once. We came to a spot in the stream that the water fell four feet over a ledge creating a small waterfall that fell into a pool of water the size of three bath tubs.

Before we knew it Todd had whipped his clothes off and

was heading into the pool. The only thing he left on was his shoes. He couldn't care less about his white butt being in full view of everyone. We all laughed at him, it was quite a sight to see. He screamed that the water was cold and then he sat under the waterfall and let the water fall unto his head. He yelled above the sound of the brook, "Isn't this purty?"

James Ernest asked, "I hope you're not talking about your butt."

Todd laughed and said, "No, the waterfall. It's purty." Todd was twelve and chubby, but not fat. The other three of us were as skinny as rails, except that Randy was beginning to develop some muscles. Todd had sandy colored hair and a pleasant look to his face. He seemed to be a fun person.

James Ernest looked at me as we walked toward the small pool. He then started removing his shirt and pants. Within a couple of minutes, we all were buck naked in the pool letting the cool water run over our heads. We sat in the water for a few minutes enjoying the break from the summer heat when I noticed a yellow stream in the water running with the flow of the brook.

"Hey, who peed in the water?" I yelled. All three of us looked at Todd who had a sheepish grin on his face.

"But I had to pee. What's wrong? It's flowing away. Look, the yellow is purty flowing away."

We started screaming, "It's purty, it's purty. You're sick," as we jumped out of the pool. I looked back at Todd and he was still sitting under the waterfall having the time of his life. The cool water had made me need to pee, so I walked behind a tree and peed. I looked around and everyone had the same idea.

We began dressing after we got dried off by the heat. Todd

was still in the water. I said to him, "Come on, Purty, let's go. Let's walk a little farther up the stream. I've never been this far."

Randy said, "He's right, Todd, time to go on Purty."

Suddenly, we had a nickname for Todd. We walked for another half hour before we turned around and started back. We talked about nothing important, but we teased each other and made fun of Todd. He just grinned. He seemed to like his new nickname.

It was well past lunch by the time we made it back to the lake and Randy and Purty decided they needed to get home and do their afternoon chores. James Ernest and I picked up our poles and bait on the way.

"We'll see you guys soon," I said as they left for home.

"I had fun," Purty said.

James Ernest and I headed for the house to have Mamaw fix us a sandwich. Mamaw asked where we had been so long, and I told her about Todd and Randy and hiking with them and what fun we had. James Ernest added, "They are two crazy guys."

Mamaw laughed as we headed for the pop cooler while she made us sandwiches. I called back for Mamaw to leave the crust on the bread. Papaw heard me and said, "Our boy is becoming a man."

James Ernest picked a Coke and I got an RC Cola. After we ate, James Ernest went home and I laid on the couch and fell asleep.

5 A PAINFULLY SLOW SAUNTER

Almost every day that week the four of us guys had hung out doing different things. Tuesday we all went fishing up on Devil's Creek. It ended up being just a big water fight. Purty was the first to pull his clothes off and go skinny dipping. Wednesday was really hot and we spent the afternoon playing cards in our living room. Mamaw made raisin cookies for everyone. Purty kept his clothes on.

Thursday, James Ernest had to paint the fence around their trailer. We all helped. I got my paintbrush from last year and James Ernest had one. We took turns painting. Purty suggested if he took his clothes off, he wouldn't get any paint on them. Taking off his shirt was as far as we let him go.

Then on Friday we spent a few hours at the Tuttle's farm; we played games in the barn. We went swimming in the new pond. Purty led the way skinny dipping again. Sadie made her way to the pond while we were swimming. We didn't see her coming. Mr. Tuttle had built a dock and James Ernest was getting ready to jump off it stark naked when Sadie said, "You boys are going to get sun burnt."

James jumped into the pond as quick as a startled frog and hid under the dock. Randy yelled, "Get out of here, Sadie."

"I might stay and watch you boys swim for a while."

"I'm warning you, Sadie."

She ignored Randy and looked at me and said, "Hi, Timmy. It's good to see you." I had tried to maneuver as far away as I could, but she started walking around the pond toward me. I didn't know how long I could tread water in the middle of the pond. My feet didn't touch the bottom.

I said, "Hi, Sadie. I think maybe you ought to go back to the house before I drown."

"I wouldn't want that to happen," she smiled. Purty started swimming toward the bank and began climbing out. He paid no attention to her. He didn't care about being naked in front of his sister or anyone else apparently. It seemed natural for Purty to run around with no clothes on. "I'll leave before you drown if you'll promise to come back this evening and take me for a walk."

I tried to think about what I should do while I was struggling to stay afloat. Finally I said, "I'll have to ask my grandparents."

"Promise me."

"Okay."

"Good. I'll see you around seven." Sadie turned around and walked away, and I quickly swam to shore before I drowned. I watched her walk away. She had on short cut-off blue jeans and a sleeveless blouse tied in a knot showing her stomach. Her dark black hair glistened in the sun.

Purty swam over close to me and said, "She likes you."

I looked at him and said, "She doesn't even know me."

"She has asked about you every evening this week."

James Ernest was still under the dock. As soon as she was back on the other side of the barn he hustled up the bank and starting throwing on his clothes over his wet body.

"She won't be back," Randy said.

James Ernest, looking scared, said, "I'm not taking any chances."

I got out and shook off all the water I could and put my clothes back on. We said goodbyes and headed down the path toward the swinging bridge. Randy yelled out, "See you guys tomorrow?"

"It's the weekend. I'll probably help around the store and lake," I explained. "I may see you tonight."

As James Ernest and I walked down the path James Ernest said, "She scares me."

"Who, Sadie?"

"Yeah, something spooky about her. I guess her looks, and the way she looks at you."

"She does act a little strange sometimes." We walked a ways and then I asked, "Are you enjoying us hanging out with Randy and Purty?"

"Yeah, Purty is a blast. I didn't know if I would like Randy at first. But he's *purty* okay." We both laughed at his joke.

"Same for me."

I walked into the back door. No one was in the kitchen. I heard Mamaw and Papaw talking to customers in the store and I made my way there.

Mrs. Loraine Tuttle was there buying some groceries. She turned and said hi to me when I walked in.

"I just got back from your farm," I told her.

"Did you have fun?" Before I could answer she continued. "Randy and Todd have really enjoyed the week. It's been so good for them to have a couple of friends to do things with. I think Sadie has a crush on you also. Mr. Tuttle and I thought you were so sweet for giving us those pictures last year. You are quite a boy. You can come up and visit just any time you want. It's so nice having a person you like so close. We'll have to have you up for dinner some evening, Timmy. In fact, we'll have all of you up for dinner some evening. Maybe I'll fix a big pork roast and potatoes. I'll let you know when…"

She talked and talked until my ears began hurting. I saw Papaw look at Mamaw and roll his eyes. When she finally paused, I told her that Sadie had wanted me to come up this evening and take her for a walk. I asked Mamaw and Papaw if that was okay. They said it was fine. I asked Mrs. Tuttle to let Sadie know I could.

"Well, that will be so nice. I'll be sure to tell her you're coming. It should be a great evening for a walk. I can't remember when the last time I've been out for a walk. It may have been last year when we still lived in Morehead. One evening, Forest and I walked up to the ice cream shop for a cone. I miss that place. It had the best soft serve cones. Have you ever had soft serve cones? They even had chocolate. I'll have to have Forest take me for a…"

I turned and walked out before my head exploded. I had grabbed an orange push-up ice cream while she was talking and I headed for my bedroom. I closed the door behind me. I didn't really want to take Sadie for a walk, but I had promised that I would. I was actually hoping my grandparents would say I couldn't. Sadie seemed nice enough and she was pretty. She was pushy though. I didn't feel at ease around her like I was with Susie.

Loraine Tuttle finally left and I heard Papaw say, "That

woman can talk. Mildred is quite a talker, but that woman could put her to shame in a talking contest."

"Now Martin, she's very nice," Mamaw said.

I heard Papaw walking through the living room whispering under his breath, "Yak, yak, yak, yak, yak, yak, yak."

I fell asleep on my bed and woke up a couple of hours later. I was hoping I had slept past time to go for the walk with Sadie. I looked at the clock and it was only half past four. I walked into the kitchen and Mamaw was frying hamburgers.

"I was just about ready to come wake you up."

"I guess I smelled the hamburgers."

"You're not the only one," Mamaw said as she motion toward the back screen door where Leo was lying against the screen with his nose in the air.

While we ate dinner we began talking about the Tuttle's. Mamaw asked how I liked having the Tuttle children nearby to play with.

"James Ernest and I have become good friends with Randy and Todd. It's a lot different than last year. I have people to talk with."

"Including James Ernest," Mamaw suggested.

"Yeah, it's really strange carrying on a conversation with James Ernest. I really like him. He's become my best friend," I explained.

"What's Randy and Todd like?" Papaw asked.

"Todd is real funny. At first I wasn't sure if I was going to like Randy, but after I got to know him, he's cool."

"How is Todd funny?"

"He likes to run around naked."

"What?" Papaw said.

"Loraine told me one day that Todd liked to take his clothes off when he can," Mamaw said.

"Was that a warning to us?" Papaw asked.

Mamaw explained, "I guess so. She said when he was around eight they were at a park letting the kids play in the playground. She said she was talking to another mother that was there with her children. She said she had turned her head for a couple of minutes and when she looked back toward her kids, Todd was hanging upside down on the monkey bars naked. All the little girls were standing looking at him and snickering. She said he was just hanging there like it was the most natural thing in the world."

Papaw commented, "If she was talking, it was probably more like an hour before she turned back around."

I added, "He does like to shed his clothes, but Purty is a lot of fun."

"What do you mean, Purty?"

"We gave him a new nickname. He's always saying how purty something is. So his nickname kind of stuck."

Papaw just nodded his head and said, "Weird family, if you ask me."

"Now Martin, every family is a little peculiar."

Papaw just nodded again, "If you say so. I'd say we should stock up on some looney pills."

Mamaw said, "Shame on you, Martin." She couldn't keep a straight face and we all laughed.

At six-thirty I told Mamaw that I was heading on up to the Tuttle's house to take Sadie for the walk like I had promised. Mamaw slicked my hair back and told me, "Be a good boy. Behave yourself."

I walked across the gravel road, over the bridge and across the new bridge that led up to the Tuttle's house. I took my time and watched the bird's flying across the meadow that ran along the lane to their house. Mr. Tuttle had put up wooden posts and a wire fence. The birds kept landing on the fence and then taking flight searching for flying bugs over the meadows weeds and flowers. The barn swallows and bluebirds stood out among the birds. Mr. Tuttle had placed a couple of bluebird houses on the fence posts. I liked them. When I got to the top of the crest I saw Sadie sitting in the porch swing. She stood up when she saw me and started walking to meet me.

She was awfully pretty. She had put on a yellow and white sundress and had a yellow head band covered with plastic flowers in her hair.

"Hi, Timmy."

"Hi, Sadie."

"Do I look pretty enough to take for a walk?"

"Yeah, I guess so."

"Where should we walk? We could go down the path to the swinging bridge, or we could walk the path toward the cabin, or we could walk back down the lane."

"Shouldn't I say hello to your family first," I suggested. I was hoping maybe Todd or someone else would want to walk with us.

"I've already told them we were leaving for our walk. Mom said for us to have fun and to be back before dark."

Dark was almost three hours away. I thought we would walk ten minutes, and I would head back to the store and maybe fish this evening.

"I know, let's walk down the lane and go to the store. I'll

buy us each a pop and some candy. Dad gave me money to pay. Then you can take me back home across the swinging bridge. That will be a nice walk."

So we started back down the lane toward the store. As we started walking, I was thinking that she could have just met me at the store and saved me from having to walk all the way up to her house. I was walking fast trying to get it over with.

"Tim, you're walking way to fast. Slow down so we can talk and enjoy the evening."

Sadie grabbed hold of my wrist and slipped her arm inside of mine. She was forcing me to walk at her pace. She then interlocked her fingers together around my arm.

"It's so nice having you here for the summer. I know we are going to get to know each other real well. You don't have a girlfriend in Ohio, do you?"

"No."

"Good," she said.

She talked on and on as we strolled down the lane toward the creek. She talked about wanting to get married as soon as she was out of school and how she wanted to have a handsome husband, like me. She said she wanted to be rich and live in Hollywood. Squirrels scampered in front of us, and birds were singing in the trees. I was paying more attention to them. It was the slowest walk I had ever been on. I'm not even sure you could call it a walk, maybe a painfully slow saunter. The only way I would have enjoyed it would have been to replace Sadie with Susie. Walks with Susie never lasted long enough.

At last we came to the creek and she made me stop to look at the water below. She said something about how water kept flowing like love between two people. At least it was something stupid like that. What did she know about love between two people? Finally we crossed the creek and headed to the store. When we turned toward the store I saw Clayton's red pickup truck in the gravel lot.

"I'm not thirsty. Let's go back the way we came. I want to see the squirrels again." I tried to turn, but her qrip tightened and I was forced to continue to the store.

When we got to the bridge in front of the store, the screen door shot open and Susie came running out and down the steps toward us. Her head was down looking where she stepped until she hit the gravel. She then looked up and saw Sadie walking beside me with her arm in mine. She stopped on a dime and stared. I looked at Susie, and started to smile and wave, when Sadie leaned into me and planted a big kiss on my cheek.

Susie turned and ran around the store and into the backyard.

"Why did you do that?" I said angrily.

"I thought you would like it."

"I didn't."

I pulled my arm away, and ran toward the store and around to the backyard looking for Susie. I didn't see her anywhere. I yelled, "Susie, Susie, where are you?" I didn't get an answer. I also didn't know what to do. Should I wait until Susie showed up? Should I go to the lake, jump in, and end it all? I thought maybe that was a little drastic. Besides, I hadn't done anything wrong. I decided to keep my promise and walk Sadie back to her house as quick as I could, then come back and look for Susie. Maybe she'd be in the house by then.

I ran back around the house and onto the front porch. Sadie

was inside buying the pops and candy. Papaw was waiting on her. I opened the door and said, "Sadie, we need to go."

"Where are going in such a hurry?" Papaw asked.

"Sadie needs to get back home."

"No, I don't. I'm not in a big hurry."

"If you want me to walk you home, we need to go now," I insisted.

Sadie looked at me like she was mad and then smiled and turned to Papaw and said, "I guess I do need to go. Thank you, Mr. Collins."

Sadie followed me off the porch. She handed me an RC Cola and a Zero candy bar. "Your grandpa said that Zero was one of your favorites. I hope he was right."

"Yes. It is."

Sadie was drinking an Orange Crush and had a Hershey's bar. She said, "I think the Orange Crush matches my sundress. What do you think?"

"I guess it does. I never really chose a pop to match what I was wearing."

We walked in silence as we walked quickly up Morgan Road toward the swinging bridge. "Is Susie mad over something?"

"I guess so," was all I could say. I could see Sadie grin out of the corner of my eye.

We continued walking in silence all the way to the bridge. When we turned to cross the bridge, Sadie said, "Susie doesn't have a right to be mad. She doesn't own you, does she?"

"No."

"She doesn't own me either. She can't tell me who I can kiss, just like she can't tell you who you can kiss." We now were in the middle of the swinging bridge. She stopped and said, "Do you want to kiss me on the lips?"

No one had ever asked me that before. I knew that I would like to kiss a girl on the lips, but not Sadie. I looked at her. "You can, if you want to," she said through her smile.

In a way, I wanted to. But in a stronger way, I didn't. I looked at her standing there in her beautiful sundress, her black hair glowing with the sun's rays shining through the limbs of the tall trees onto her head. I saw the plastic flowers in her hair. She moistened her lips and puckered them and I...ran.

"You know your way home from here," I yelled back toward her as I ran harder. I had my empty pop bottle in one hand and a candy wrapper in the other, and they both were pumping up and down as I ran as fast as I could.

I heard her yell something, but I couldn't understand her for the gravel sounds as they scattered in the wake of my running away.

I ran all the way to the store. Clayton and Papaw were sitting on the front porch whittling with Leo between them. I waved and said hello as I ran past them and through the front door to the store. I heard Papaw say, "Looks like he's in a hurry. I wonder where he left Sadie."

The twins were playing with Barbie dolls in the living room. Delma stood up to say something, but I flew past her and into the kitchen. Monie and Mamaw were breaking green beans and Susie was no where in sight. I stopped long enough to ask where Susie was. Monie said, "She said she wanted to walk back to the swimming hole. I didn't want her to walk up there by herself, so she said she would just walk around the lake."

I quickly ran through the backyard and up to the dam. I

stopped and looked down both sides of the lake, but didn't see her. It was getting pretty dark around the lake by then with the hills blocking the sunset. I ran around the west side of the lake and up and down both rises. As I was running down the last rise I saw Susie sitting on the slanted rock. She sat looking out into the lake.

"I've been looking for you," I said. I saw her hand go up to her face and wipe something away.

"I wanted to be alone and look at the lake," she answered,

Susie was sitting at my favorite spot. Last year at this same spot she had fallen into the lake backward when her hand slipped off mine because night crawler scum was on my hand.

I sat down beside her. I didn't know what to say, so I just sat there quietly. She still hadn't looked at me. After about ten minutes I said, "I only went for a walk with Sadie because I had to."

She looked at me confused.

I continued, not knowing any better, "Randy, Todd, James Ernest, and I were skinny dipping in their pond when Sadie snuck up on us."

I was hoping this would help. "She said she wasn't going to leave until I promised to take her for a walk this evening." I stood up in front of her and continued, "I was in the middle of the pond ready to drown, so I said okay."

Susie stood up. I thought she was going to hug me and forgive me. Her hands reached toward my chest—and she pushed me as hard as she could and I toppled backward into the lake. She screamed, "Maybe this time you will drown!"

I hit my hand on a rock as I fell and I grabbed it and then shook it. It was scraped badly and blood started showing. Susie angrily said, "If you're hurt, you might be in luck, Sadie would probably be glad to kiss it and make it better." With that said, she turned, jumped off the slanted rock and ran toward the house.

I stood up and the water was up to my chest. At that moment I wanted the water to be over my head. I knew that Susie was really mad at me, and she probably wouldn't want to talk to me for a long time, if ever. I just stood there for a long time and held my bleeding hand under the water. It was a good thing the lake didn't have sharks.

I slowly made my way out of the lake. I decided not to go back to the house for a while. I didn't want to face Susie or the twins. I walked back onto the rock and sat down and listened to the darkness come on the lake. The sounds of the lake changed when dusk came. Different birds called from their spots in the trees. Sometimes you would see an owl fly across the lake in the moon light. Bull frogs croaked on the banks. Bats swooped at anything that moved. Sounds echoed around the lake and every little sound could be heard that you would normally miss in the daylight.

I sat there wishing Susie wasn't mad at me. I wished we could listen to the spectacular night sounds together. A full moon rose over the eastern hillside and lit up the small ripples on the lake from the light breeze that blew down the lake toward me. I wondered what Susie told everyone when she returned to the house without me. I wasn't sure if she would tell everyone about Sadie kissing me or not. I never have trouble like this when I just play with the guys. After another half hour I decided I had better head to the house so Mamaw and

Papaw wouldn't worry. My hand had stopped bleeding, and I would hide it behind my back when I walked in.

When I walked into the kitchen Mamaw asked where I had been. I told her, "I watched the moon rise over the lake." Monie was still sitting at the table with Mamaw. The twins and Susie were sitting on the couch watching TV. I walked past them and went into my bedroom and shut the door. I changed into dry underwear and went to bed. It hadn't been one of my favorite days.

6 THE BROKEN TOE

I had spent the weekend doing chores around the store and lake. The pay lake was filled with fishermen and the store was filled with shoppers. We sold lots of bait and snacks to the fishermen and sandwiches at lunchtime. The weather was really nice. The high was only going to be near eighty both days with a nice breeze. I mowed the yard Saturday afternoon and walked to the spring for a bucket of fresh water.

James Ernest walked with me to the spring and helped carry the pail. I told James Ernest about Sadie and Susie. He said it must be nice having two girls like me. I told him it wasn't. I explained that I only wanted one of them to like me. I then told him about Sadie trying to get me to kiss her on the lips and how I had run. He said he didn't blame me. He said he would have flown away if he could. James Ernest said he was still a little scared of Sadie.

Sunday afternoon I heard Loraine Tuttle and Sadie in the store talking to Mamaw. Sadie asked if I was there. So I ran out the back door, up to the lake and hid. James Ernest and I fished a little Sunday evening near dark. James Ernest never had to pay to fish since he was my friend. After breakfast and chores, Papaw asked if I wanted to go to West Liberty with him. Of course I said yes. I went into the bank with Papaw and said hello to Mr. Harney the banker. When we went to the general store Papaw asked, "Is there anything you would like for helping out around the store?"

"I would like a Wiffle bat and a couple of balls. The four of us guys have talked about starting a Wiffleball league, but we need the bats and balls."

"Pick out a couple of bats and a few balls. You may go through them pretty fast," Papaw said.

I picked out a slender yellow bat and a bat that was a little fatter. I got four wiffle balls. Two of the four had holes. I knew we guys could make the balls with holes do funny things when you pitched it. When we got back to the house I called Randy and Purty and told them about the bats and balls. They said they would come down after lunch and we could start the league games. I ran up to tell James Ernest. He said okay.

My great Aunt Ruby and Uncle Homer were there when I returned. Everyone was sitting in the living room and Papaw asked me to watch the store for a while. Ruby was a very small lady, less than five feet tall with a small frame. Homer was a husky white-haired gentleman with a large white mustache. They always seemed to be together. I wasn't sure how old they were, except that I knew they were about the same age as my grandparents. Uncle Homer was Mamaw's brother.

I heard Ruby say something about Uncle Morton. I couldn't make out what she said. A customer walked through the front door. It was one of the fishermen from the pay pond. He picked out a box of crackers and a can of Vienna sausages. He grabbed a bottle of RC Cola from the cooler and asked me to get him a cup of night crawlers. As I walked through the living room I noticed concern on everyone's faces. No one said anything as I passed by.

The gentleman paid and then a pretty lady with a little child came in. I wanted to listen to the conversation in the living room, but the kid started talking to me.

"What's your name?"

"I'm Timmy. What's your name?"

"Bobby Lee Simmons. How old are you?"

"I'm ten. I'll be eleven next month. How old are you Bobby Lee?"

The mother was bringing items to the counter while I talked to her son. "I'm four. I'll be five next year. Are you married?"

I laughed and then answered, "No. I'm still too young."

"My mom ain't married either."

His mother quickly added, "I don't think Timmy is interested in my marriage situation, Bobby Lee."

"Does your dad live here?" Bobby Lee asked.

"No."

Before I could explain he said, "My dad doesn't live with me either. I don't know my dad. Do you have a girlfriend?"

"I don't know. I did, kind of."

"Did she find someone else?"

"Bobby Lee, you're being way too nosy for your own good. Good Lord, Bobby Lee, sometimes you can embarrass me to death. I'm sorry, Timmy. Bobby Lee gets carried away. He's never met a stranger."

"That's okay. I like to talk, also."

"I'm Miss Rebecca Simmons." She reached out her hand and I shook it. "I just moved into the area, and this is my first time here. Bobby Lee and I moved into the farmhouse on top of the hill next to the Clayton Perry farm."

"That's a nice place. Are you going to farm it?"

"Heaven's no. I'm just renting the house for now. I work in West Liberty at the Bank. I'm a secretary there."

"You know Mr. Harney then."

"Yes. He's my boss. He's a very nice man. You'll have to come up and visit Bobby Lee and me. I'm sure Bobby Lee has a bushel load of questions for you."

"I have one for Bobby Lee."

"Okay," Bobby Lee stood with his eyes wide open.

"Do you like big suckers?"

"I sure do."

I took one of the biggest suckers out of one the large glass jars that sat on the counter and handed it to him. He smiled and quickly tore the wrapper off.

"Bobby Lee, what do you say?"

"Thank you."

Miss Rebecca Simmons paid for her two bags of groceries, and I helped her to her car by carrying one of the bags.

"Ain't you the sweetest thing? Thank you. You come visit us, hear? We'll be back when we need something else." Bobby Lee jumped into the front seat with his sweet attractive mother and waved with his empty hand.

I had forgotten about the conversation going on in the living room until I returned inside. Papaw and Homer were inside the store now and Mamaw and Ruby were in the kitchen fixing sandwiches for lunch. I decided not to ask about it until Homer and Ruby left or until this evening.

I liked Miss Rebecca and Bobby Lee. I decided that I

would have to walk up and visit them some evening. I ate lunch and went outside to set up the baseball field. We actually didn't have a field. I outlined a strike zone on the shed and marked a spot for the pitching rubber. We were going to play one person against another. The other two would be umpires. We also would have teams of two against two. The rules were if you hit the ball past the pitcher it would be a single, past the well on a fly was a double, past the driveway up the dam on a fly was a home run. For now we had no triples. Pitchers could pitch as hard as they wanted. The umpires would determine if a pitch hit inside the strike zone or if the batter swung. Each team had to pick a major league team to be, and they had to hit the same as the players for that team, if we knew for sure which way they batted.

I was going to try to be either the Cincinnati Reds or the Boston Red Sox. I knew every player on the Reds and which way they batted. I would bat left-handed when Vada Pinson was up and right-handed when Frank Robinson was at bat and so on.

James Ernest arrived first and I showed him the bats and balls. He was excited. We practiced a while before Randy and Purty showed up. We decided since this was the first game that we all would play and the pitcher would call the balls and strikes. Purty and I ended up being the Reds and Randy and James Ernest decided to be the Yankees. We flipped for home team. Randy won the coin toss.

Randy pitched for his team. We decided that when we played two on a team that if a player caught a fly ball it was an out even if it was hit past the home run mark. Randy was the biggest and strongest of us and threw the ball hard. I batted first and led off as Roy McMillan and promptly struck out on four pitches. Purty struck out on three pitches batting like Billy Martin. I was up again and got to hit like Vada Pinson. Randy tried to throw a knuckleball with two strikes, and I hit it high over the home run mark.

Purty wanted to pitch for us and James Ernest and Randy got hit after hit off of him. Purty said he had a great change up, and that's all he threw. We got beat 21 to 4. It was great fun though. We took a break and sat under a tree in the shade. Papaw asked if we wanted some lemonade, and everyone did. I ran into the kitchen and helped Mamaw with the plastic glasses and the pitcher. "I'll leave the pitcher here in case you boys want refills."

As we were drinking Randy said, "I've been thinking. We ought to start a club. We could come up with a name and maybe build a clubhouse."

James Ernest got excited and said, "Yeah, good idea. I like it."

Purty chipped in, "How about The Four Musketeers?"

Randy said, "No. That's stupid."

Purty had another suggestion, "How about The Robin Hoods?"

We all said, "No."

"We'll think of a name later. We need to have an official meeting—but where?" Randy asked.

"How about the cabin?" I recommended.

James Ernest and Randy looked at each other and nodded and Randy said, "Good idea. That can be our clubhouse until we get one built."

Purty suggested, "Every club has to have an initiation for the members."

We all thought about it. Todd was right. We had to come up with something.

Purty was first with a suggestion, "How about everyone has to run around the lake on a Saturday—naked."

We laughed because we knew if it was his idea it would be something having to do with running around naked.

Randy finally said, "I got it."

We all looked at him anxiously. "What?" I asked.

He looked at each of us, one by one, and then said, "We meet tonight, at midnight, at the cabin. To be in the club, you have to be there. We'll come up with a club name and motto." He stared at each of us again. No one wanted to say they didn't want to do it. We all wanted to be in the club. He added, "Part of it is, you can't ask permission and you can't tell anyone where you've been if you get caught. Club secret."

Randy looked at me and asked, "You in?"

"Yes," I answered.

"Yes," Todd said.

"No problem, I'll be there," James Ernest said.

Randy said, "I'll bring a pad and pencil for rules and things we want to write down. Timmy, bring some matches so we can build a fire. Todd and I will meet you guys there at midnight. If someone doesn't show up, he's out of the club—no excuses. One other thing, think of ideas that we can vote on for the club."

James Ernest said he would meet me at eleven fifteen at the beginning of Morgan Road.

All the guys went home. I walked into the store and got a creamsicle. I moseyed into the kitchen. Mamaw and Papaw were sitting at the table talking. They quit when I walked in. I asked, "So what's wrong with Uncle Morton."

They both just stared at me. Mamaw started to cry. Papaw finally answered, "He's having some health problems."

"What kind of health problems?"

"Apparently he's having a lot of numbness in both arms and tingling in his left arm. His hearing is getting real bad. The doctor has run tests, but he hasn't found anything. They guess that his heart might be giving out. They also think that something might be affecting his blood circulation. As of now, they're unsure, they say they've done all they can do," Papaw explained.

"So what happens now?" I asked.

Mamaw said, "We pray for him."

Papaw added, "We need to get him to agree to stay with someone until hopefully he's better. He might hurt himself in his condition."

I suggested, "He can have my room."

Mamaw asked, "What would you do?"

"I can sleep on the couch or sleep in my tent. I really don't mind. I just want Uncle Morton to get well."

"That's very kind of you. We've been talking to Homer and Ruby about him moving in with one of us. We even said he could split time in both houses."

"Of course he's hard-headed and says he'll be fine in his own house. He won't listen to us," Mamaw explained.

A customer opened the front screen door and Papaw got up to wait on them. I told Mamaw, "I sure hope they find out what's wrong with him."

"Me too."

I went into my bedroom and closed the door. I thought I might try to take a nap so I would be awake for the midnight meeting. I prayed for Uncle Morton the best I could. I laid on the bed with the fan blowing air on me. I tried to sleep, but all I could think of was Uncle Morton. I thought about how Uncle Morton believed God took away his eyesight so he could really see. I wondered what God was teaching him by taking away his hearing, his arm and maybe his heart. I wondered if Uncle Morton thought God was doing this to him.

I wanted to go talk to Uncle Morton. I walked out of my room. I couldn't sleep anyway. I walked into the store and Papaw was finishing up with a fisherman who was going to fish this evening.

"Can you take me to visit Uncle Morton this evening, Papaw?"

"We can do that."

"What time?"

"After dinner."

So after dinner Papaw took me up to Uncle Morton's to visit. It seemed like we never visited people, they always visited us. We knocked on his door, but no one answered. The front door was open, so we opened the screen door and walked in. Papaw called out, "Morton, you've got company."

There was no answer. We walked into the kitchen and Uncle Morton was sitting on the floor. A big ceramic mixing bowl was in the middle of the floor. I ran over to Uncle Morton. He jumped a little when he realized someone was there.

"Who is it?" Uncle Morton asked.

"It's Timmy and Papaw," I answered.

"What's happened in here?" Papaw loudly asked.

"I'm afraid I might have broken my big toe. I was carrying that big bowl. I lost the handle on it and it dropped right on my toe. I've been sitting here waiting for the pain to subside a little."

"How long have you been sitting here?" We were pretty much yelling to get him to hear us.

"Probably 'bout an hour. The pain doesn't want to go away."

"Let's get you up and get you to the doctor," Papaw said.

"You can help me up. But you know they can't do anything for a broken toe. He'll just tell me to stay off of it for a while and then charge me ten dollars."

"You're probably right," Papaw said as we helped pull Uncle Morton up and helped him to his favorite chair.

The broken toe may have turned out to be a blessing. He couldn't very well argue about staying with someone for a while since he couldn't walk. He agreed to stay with us for a few days. Papaw packed a small suitcase with some of his clothes. We found a bag and packed up his toothbrush and comb and other things that Papaw thought he would need. We got him into the truck which was really an ordeal. I rode in the truck bed.

When we got to the house Uncle Morton kept insisting that he would sleep on the couch. He said that the bedroom was mine. I finally convinced him to take the bedroom when I told him it was the only way my grandparents would let me sleep in the tent. I winked at Mamaw, and he finally agreed to take the bedroom. I went out back and put up the tent. I then realized that this would make it easier to sneak away for the midnight meeting. It was already dark out and I had to get matches and my flashlight. I also needed my pillow and alarm clock which

I seldom used. I set the alarm for eleven o'clock in case I fell asleep.

7 SECRETS

TUESDAY, JUNE 14

The full moon was bright and you could see really well without the flashlight, but I took it anyway. I bought a box of matches in the store without Papaw knowing about it. If I'd just asked him for some I didn't know what to tell him I needed the matches for, and I didn't want to steal them. I waited at the road for James Ernest. He was a couple of minutes late when I heard him running around the house toward me.

He motioned for me to run with him, so I did. We ran for a hundred yards or so and finally slowed to a walk.

"What was that all about?"

"You won't believe what just happened."

I didn't know, but I was plenty excited to find out.

"What?"

He explained while trying to catch his breath, "I thought I should go by your window to make sure you were awake. The moonlight was shining on your bed and I saw you laying in your bed with your back to me. I whispered your name, but you didn't bulge so I whispered again. Still nothing, so I picked up a couple of small pebbles and threw them at you."

"Oh, no, you didn't."

"I did."

"Your Uncle Morton said, 'Hey!' and rolled over and looked

me in the face. Scared me to death. I almost screamed. I ducked and ran around the house and here I am."

I laughed all the way past the swinging bridge as I told him about Uncle Morton. James Ernest couldn't help but laugh also once the fright was gone.

"I wonder what Uncle Morton thought. He probably thought he was having a nightmare," I said.

"He'll know it wasn't when he wakes up with pebbles in his bed." We both laughed again.

We walked to where the cut off was. We crossed the creek by shining the flashlight on the rocks that made a path. We followed the small trail along the west side of the creek to the wide trail that led through the woods to the cabin. This was the same way I had come last summer when I followed the Tattoo Man to his cabin. The anxious moments and memories were flooding back.

James Ernest and I walked along the path in silence. The moon shone through the treetops and lit the trail enough to see our way. We heard tree frogs and nightingales in the woods as we walked. An owl flew across the trail right in front of us and scared both of us. We stopped and waited for a second.

"I wonder what kind of owl that was," I asked.

"Probably a Great Horned Owl," James Ernest said.

I just looked at him. I wondered if he really knew or if he had just heard that name before. I didn't ask. We came to the trail that ran south to the Tuttle Farm. We looked down the trail to see if Randy and Todd were on it. We didn't see or hear anything. We kept walking. I heard something walking toward us in the distance. I grabbed James Ernest's arm and pulled him off the trail behind a tree.

"Quiet, something's coming," I whispered.

We stood quiet, peeking around the tree. The sound got closer and closer until we could see a porcupine and three babies scurrying behind. A baby smelled us and moved in close to us. James Ernest kicked the dirt in front of its nose, and that sent all of them running up the trail away from us.

We continued down the trail toward the cabin. When we got to the end of the trail, we turned right. This led to the cabin. We didn't see any activity at the meeting spot. We decided to try and build a fire. I walked around the cabin and found a fire pit already built with kindling and logs ready to light.

I called James Ernest over and we looked at it. Who would have built this? Four rocks had been placed around the pit. I looked at my watch and it was ten minutes after midnight. "You think they're going to show up?" I asked.

"It's not going to be much of a club with only two members," James Ernest said. "Sadie would join for you." He made a pucker mouth as he drug out *you*.

"Funny man, you're a real funny man."

"We could call the club the 'Kissy Club' and the initiation would be—you have to kiss Timmy," James Ernest added.

"I think I liked you better when you didn't talk." We laughed.

"What are you guys laughing about?" We heard Randy ask as he walked into the clearing of the cabin.

"Where have you guys been? You're late. We were starting to come up with a club for two guys."

"I couldn't get purty boy awake enough to get him out of bed. It took forever."

"I like sleeping. I was dreaming about hitchhiking down the highway naked as a jaybird."

"He sleeps in the nude and he had to get dressed once I got him up and awake. Let's light the fire," Randy said.

"How did you know about the pit," I asked.

Randy explained that he had come to the cabin after dinner and built it. He said he thought it would be hard to find everything in the dark—pretty smart. We built a small fire. We decided it would be too hot if we made it too big, since it was still in the seventies.

We each picked a spot around the pit. I sat across from Purty with Randy on my left and James Ernest on my right, each facing the other. I shared the story about Uncle Morton staying with us and James Ernest trying to wake him up. We all laughed. I already knew this club would be tremendous fun.

"Okay, I think we should make club rules," Randy said.

"I have an idea. All rules have to be voted on," I hesitated and then added, "Every rule and decision has to be voted unanimously to apply."

"Why not by majority instead?" Todd asked.

"Because someone may be totally against something, and we don't want someone to feel bad about something, or quit the club because of a rule," I explained.

Randy said, "Let's vote on it." We all voted to accept the unanimous vote. Randy wrote it down.

James Ernest said, "We need a president and I think it should be Randy. The club was his idea and he's the oldest." We all voted for Randy.

Purty suggested, "Let's call it something other than president."

"How about Leader?" I said.

James Ernest got all excited and almost yelled out in his deep voice, "Leader of the Pack. Our club could be The Pack and Randy could be the Leader of the Pack."

Purty jumped up and said, "I like it, I like it. We could even be the Wolf Pack."

At the same time we all jumped up and started chanting, "The Wolf Pack, the Wolf Pack, the Wolf Pack," as the smoke rose up through the middle of our club. We then settled down and voted for the name, the Wolf Pack, and for Randy to be called the Leader unanimously.

Randy then said, "I have another rule to vote on. If a member tells the club a secret or says he doesn't want something told, it then stays among us forever. If someone breaks this rule he will be forever kicked out and forever shamed." We all agreed.

Purty then said, "Another rule—no girls." We all said, "Yes, yes, yes, and yes."

Randy then asked, "You do mean, no girls in the Wolf Pack as members, don't you."

"Yes. What else would I mean?"

"I was hoping you didn't mean, no girlfriends forever, as one of our rules." We all laughed until it hurt.

James Ernest then said, "Wait, if our initiation is getting naked, we might want girls in the club."

We all laughed again. I couldn't believe James Ernest had said that, the same James Ernest that had not spoken for eight years. Here he was cracking jokes and laughing about naked girls.

When the laughter died down I said, "I think we should have a rule that says we can change a rule or add a rule any time we feel necessary by vote. That way if we find a girl that will do a naked initiation, we can change the rules." Everyone agreed and laughed even harder.

Randy then asked, "Has anyone thought of a club motto? Something like, 'One for all and all for one.' I've always liked that one."

Purty suggested, "Tea for two and two for tea." We laughed harder again and I thought Randy was going to throw Purty into the fire.

I then said, "How about, 'Forever the Pack?'"

Everyone thought about it.

"I like it. It's simple and to the point," James Ernest said.

Randy said, "I do too."

Purty grinned and said, "I guess it will do if we can't have 'tea for two and…'" Randy and James Ernest both jumped on him and started playfully hitting him about his body before he could finish. "I can only think of one more rule for now. We can always add others as we need them," Randy said.

"What's the other one?" I asked.

"The initiation."

We all got quiet and listened to Randy. It felt as though he was giving us the deep secret of life. We leaned in closer to the fire to hear what we had to do. I could see the reflection of the burning embers in each guy's eyes.

"Tonight," he stated, "each of us must tell the Wolf Pack a secret or something they have done that they are ashamed of, or never wanted to tell anyone else about. It can be something stupid or totally bad. This will seal our trust to keep things between us. This thing that you tell us must not be known by anyone else except a person that you may have done it to."

We all look at each other and I said, "Should we take a vote to see if everyone agrees to the initiation?" We agreed that we should vote and we all agreed to the initiation.

Randy then said, "We'll wait a few minutes to think of what we want to tell." We waited for a long time. I tried to decide what I should tell. My first thought was the Indian cave. I quickly knew that I couldn't. That was a secret I had with Susie, and I couldn't break it. Although, I thought holding our club meetings inside the cave where the Indians may have held theirs would be neat. After a while Randy asked, "Is everyone ready?" Everyone nodded yes. "Who wants to go first?"

James Ernest raised his hand, "I'll go. Last summer, I was almost positive that the Tattoo Man killed Mrs. Robbins. The day he killed her, I saw him walking toward her house. I didn't see him do it, but I saw him. I also watched him break out all the windows of the police cars when Timmy led the police to the cabin. I wanted to go with them; I ran up to the farm trying to catch up, when I got there the Tattoo Man had a big wooden stick busting every window and light. Of course I never told anyone because I wouldn't talk. I figured they knew who busted the windows anyway."

No one said a word. Just thinking about the Tattoo Man ran shivers through my bones. Sitting outside in the dark at midnight around the fire seemed to make it worse. My body was shaking even though we were sitting next to the fire on a summer night. I saw Purty looking over his shoulder into the trees.

Randy then said, "That was a good one. I'll go next."

Randy squirmed on his rock and then started, "This spring our Aunt Elizabeth visited us for a few days. She's our mom's youngest sister. She's nineteen and very beautiful. She wanted to take a bath, and our tub is on the back screen porch. Dad told Todd and me to go to do chores and stay away from the house for at least an hour. Dad left and went to town."

We all sat there with anticipation as to where this confession was heading. He continued, "Todd was cleaning out the cow stalls and I was putting fresh hay in the chicken coop. I decided to sneak over to the porch. I slowly raised my head over the windowsill to look through the screen. She was standing in the tub, drying off with her back to me, completely naked except for the towel. I watched her for maybe ten seconds and then she glanced toward where I was and I ducked and ran as fast as I could."

We all just sat there. No one could say a word.

"The strange thing was, I really enjoyed looking at her for the moment, but I began feeling ashamed that I had done that to my aunt."

Then out of the blue Purty asked, "When is she coming back to visit?"

I laughed until my sides hurt. James Ernest had tears coming down his face from laughter. Randy just looked at Purty.

"What? I've never seen a naked woman."

The laughter didn't die down for a long time.

We were finally able to stop laughing and I said, "I'll go next. Mine isn't as good as you guys. I took one of my dad's cigarettes from his pack one day while he was drunk and went to the garage and tried to smoke it."

James Ernest said, "I've done that."

"Me too," Randy said.

Todd raised his hand and shook his head yes showing that he had done that also.

"I took one puff and gagged on it and threw it away. I wondered why people smoked. It was awful," I explained.

Todd said, "Dad doesn't smoke, but we took a couple from our Uncle Sid, and we got caught. Dad made us smoke the whole pack until we were so sick we both threw up for an hour. I was in bed for a whole day. No more smoking for me."

"Let's make a Pack rule that we never smoke again," I suggested. Everyone agreed and Randy got out the pad and wrote it down.

It was Todd's turn. I was sure his would have something to do with being naked, but it didn't. His was much worse.

Purty said as a matter of fact, "I tried to talk Sadie into playing *spin the bottle* with me."

We all looked at him and then it hit us that he was talking about his sister.

"Gross! You sicko!" James Ernest yelled.

"That's the worst thing yet!" I yelled.

Randy said, "Our sister?"

We all got him down on the ground and started beating lightly on him. He laughed and laughed. We let him up and I said, "You know Purty, if it was just the two of you, you were actually just asking your sister to make out with you." Everyone laughed and agreed, including Purty.

The initiation was over and Randy as Leader declared us, "Officially the Wolf Pack."

"Before we leave I thought of something. I think we need a club handshake or chant or something. What do you guys think?" I asked.

James Ernest said he had an idea. He had us stand in a circle and howl to the sky like wolves. We then jumped up and down four times chanting, "Wolf Pack, Wolf Pack, Wolf Pack, Wolf Pack." One chant for each member in the club. We then held out our hands in the middle like a basketball team and we yelled, "Forever the Pack."

Purty asked if it would be better in the nude. "No!"

Everyone loved it, except the nude part, and we voted it in.

I looked at my watch and it was three o'clock and by the time we could get home it would be close to four. We decided that the first meeting of the Wolf Pack was over. Randy said he would let us know when the next meeting would be.

We put the fire out by covering it with dirt and smothering it. We all headed together down the trail away from the cabin. At the turn off we said goodbye and Randy said they would see us tomorrow afternoon to play Wiffleball.

On the way home James Ernest said, "That was the most fun I've ever had in my life." I almost agreed, if it hadn't been for showing Susie the cave.

8 A Soft Whimpering

The week was spent doing chores and helping in the store in the mornings and playing Wiffleball in the afternoons with the guys. We went to the swimming hole on Thursday after Wiffleball. The weather had turned really hot and the water felt great. It seemed like I never had any time to myself with having so many friends nearby. I missed hiking alone and exploring the mountains. Mainly, I missed Susie. I still hadn't talked to her since she pushed me into the lake.

I knew I would see her Sunday at church, but I was hoping to see her this weekend. Mamaw suggested I call her and apologize. I felt that I had nothing to apologize for. I was thinking that she would probably get over being mad and we would go back to normal. That's the way Mom and Dad did it.

Uncle Morton was still hobbling around and he could barely hear a thing. He was hard to talk to, and you sure couldn't use sign language. He was leaving this evening and going to stay with Homer and Ruby for a couple of days since the store gets hectic on weekends. I was glad to get my bed back, even if it was for just a couple of nights. The tent was uncomfortable and I had even slept on the couch one night.

It was close to two in the afternoon and I decided to go hiking by myself. The Tuttle Family was going away for the weekend to visit relatives in Indiana, and James Ernest, apparently, was resting this afternoon, so I was on my own.

Mamaw said, "Be back for supper around six. Company is coming this evening."

"Who's coming?" I wanted it to be Clayton and Monie and the girls.

"I'm not sure who all is coming. Janice called and said to expect visitors tonight. That's all she would say." I slipped out the back door and decided to walk up to the cave and hike around up there. I hadn't been back to the big cave opening that summer. I walked around the lake and up the stream to the swimming hole. I climbed up the hill to the top of the cliff and looked over the rim to the swimming hole below. I thought about last summer, and how I had discovered the cave entrance.

I turned and walked over to the three boulders that still stood guarding the hole that led down into the cave. I was surprised that no one had blocked the entrance after they pulled the dead body of the Tattoo Man out of the cave. I guess the bats wouldn't be able to get out if they had. I crawled over to the hole and looked down into the cavern and remembered hearing the Tattoo Man yelling for help. I remembered throwing the pebbles and dirt into his mouth. The whole summer of '59 flashed back while I lay there on my stomach and peered down.

I laid there and thought of how different this summer had been. I now have three friends who talk to me. Last year I was alone except for the time I spent with Susie and the few times with James Ernest. I finally got up and walked back down the hill and continued up the stream past Robert's farm and then past the small waterfall that Purty had sat naked under. I was now getting into an area that I had never been.

I hiked on looking at all the new sights. Soon I came to more cliffs. They weren't high cliffs, but fairly low overhangs covered with moss and dead trees that had fallen. Bird nests were in the crevices of the rock walls. I was looking into one of the nests when I heard something. I couldn't make out what it was at first. It sounded like a soft whimpering crying sound. But where was it coming from. Was there a house nearby? I didn't think so. I stood as still as I could and listened. Again I heard it. It sounded like it was coming from the rock wall, from the bottom of the overhang.

I got down on my hands and knees and began following the small cry. I began imitating the sound. It got a little stronger. I crawled no more than ten feet when I saw an opening going into the bottom of the wall. A small hole led to something. The hole was only maybe eighteen inches round. I put my ear up close to it and made a whimpering mimic. The sound came back almost like an echo, but it wasn't. I knew something was just inside the hole, but it was dark inside, and I couldn't see anything.

I had told myself that I would not be stupid this year. Last year I got trapped in the cave and thought I would die there. Whatever was in the hole didn't sound dangerous and I still didn't really think it was safe to stick my hand inside. But I did anyway.

I slid my hand in slowly with my fingers made into a fist. My thinking was it would be harder to bite a hand off than a finger. I got my hand in as far as I could get it. My shoulder was up against the wall. Suddenly something rubbed against my hand. It was wet and I quickly jerked my hand out. It scared the living daylights out of me. I looked at my hand to make sure everything was there.

I was okay. So I decided to put my hand back inside. This time my hand didn't make it as far in until I felt the same thing. I started to jerk it out, but didn't. I slowly brought my hand out and the wet lick continued. As my hand neared the opening I saw two eyes peering out through the dark. I wondered what was looking at me and licking my hand. I thought about talking to it, but I decided it would probably just scare it. As I pulled my hand out, the eyes hesitated. I slowly put my hand back in and enticed it to come on out. Soon the small hairy face emerged from the dark into the light.

It was a puppy, a small, helpless, starving, skinny little pup. I picked it up in both hands and held it to my chest. It was shaking against my body and its eyes looked up into mine. I wondered if there were more of them. I put my ear against the opening and made the crying sound again. No other sound came from the den. The pup in my arms cried again. I knew that the pup was starving and that I needed to give him food soon or he would probably die. I stood up and hurried out from under the overhang and started back down the stream toward the lake. I looked down at the pup. He was tan, black and brown mix with small white spots on his face and body.

As I neared Robert's farm I wondered if I should go there to get food instead of walking another thirty minutes or more to the store. I determined I should. I just prayed they would be home. Even if they weren't, the house would be unlocked, and I would be able to find something to feed it. I headed across the fields to the farm house.

Where was the mother of this pup? What kind of puppy

was it? Were there more of them in the den? I should get my flashlight and go back to look.

I looked in the shed where their workshop was. No one was there. I walked on to the house, and as I neared the house I yelled, "Is anyone home?"

Janice came out the back door and said, "Hi, Timmy. What are doing here?" Before I could answer she said, "What in the world have you got there? What is that in your arms?"

"It's a puppy. I think it needs food real bad. Do you have anything?"

"Well, I'll be. That is a puppy. Come on in. I'll get a baby bottle and we're put some milk in it. Robert! Robert! Come see what Timmy has."

Robert must have been on the front porch and he quickly came through the door and into the kitchen. "Where did you find that?"

"I heard him crying under a ledge back along the stream. He crawled out of the den when he heard me." I didn't tell them about sticking my hand inside. "He seems to be starving. I think the mother abandoned it."

"It looks like it's in pretty bad shape. It's probably a coyote pup." I hadn't even suspected that. I quickly thought about the two coyotes that I saw last summer and whether they could be the parents. "You should just let it die."

"No! I couldn't do that."

"Timmy, you could leave it here, and I'll do away with it for you. We can put it out of its misery."

"It just needs food," I said through my tears. I couldn't just let a puppy die that I might be able to save, even if it was a coyote pup. "I'm not going to save it just to kill it."

Janice returned after finding a small baby bottle. I watched her fill it with milk, and she handed it to me. Robert said, "Timmy, I really think we need to get rid of it before you get attached."

"Thanks," I said as I turned and ran out the back door and through the yard to the field and toward the trail along the stream.

"Timmy! Timmy!" I heard Robert and Janice both call my name as I ran across the field.

I stopped once I got to the woods and bent down to my knees and tried to give the puppy some milk. I held the bottle to the puppy's mouth and it opened its mouth, but he wouldn't suck.

"God, help me! The pup needs food. Help!" I turned the bottle up so a few drops would drip into its lips and the puppy did lick the milk from its lips. I did it again, and again it licked. I tried letting a drop dangle from the nipple of the bottle and the pup took the nipple into its mouth and began sucking. The puppy sucked and sucked the milk from the bottle. Tears came again to my eyes, but this time it was from the happiness of seeing the pup take the milk as I held one in each hand.

When the puppy had finished all that it was going to drink I got up and began walking slowly to the store. As I walked home, I wondered if the pup was a boy or a girl. I knew of only one way to tell, so I turned it over and looked. It was a boy pup. Good. He would be allowed to join our club, the Wolf Pack.

What would Papaw say about the pup? Would he feel the same way Robert did? I wondered if I should hide the pup. I couldn't do that. I would have to plead my case and hope that Mamaw and Papaw would let me tend it back to health. I wanted to keep it. I had never had a dog of my own. What would I name it? I was thinking too far in advance.

I arrived at the lake and walked around the west side toward the house. As I started down the last rise, ahead of me stood Billy Taulbee and his two friends, the short one and the tall one. I had not seen them this summer. I had heard they were working now. I certainly hadn't missed them.

Billy was the worst fisherman in Kentucky and always trying to give me a hard time. He looked up and saw me walking toward them. He saw the baby bottle before I could hide it and he said, "Are you feeding your baby?"

When I got up to them Billy said, "You had a baby, and it looks just like you."

I wasn't in the mood for them so I kept on walking. Finally Billy said, "Puppy got your tongue." His buddies thought his stupid joke was funny and they laughed and laughed.

As I began to walk off the dam to the house I realized that Mamaw and Papaw might not let me keep the pup. I could hide him, but Robert had probably already called to tell them about it. I was sure it would come up that evening when Robert and Janice came to visit. I figured I could tell them I decided to let it go and say that Robert was right, but I didn't want to lie to my grandparents.

I decided to take a chance that they would let me take care of it, at least until it was able to be on its own, if it was a coyote. I slowly walked into the backyard. Mamaw came out of the back screen door and said, "Papaw wants to talk to you." She looked down at the puppy, but didn't say anything. "Supper will be in a few minutes."

I sat in the grass and placed the puppy next to me. His legs were wobbly and he curled up next to my leg and lay down. He tilted his head up and looked into my eyes. I rubbed his head as he rested. Soon Papaw came out of the door and walked over to me.

"Robert called and said you were bringing a coyote pup home." He bent down to look at it. "I'm sorry, but you can't keep it."

I looked up at my grandfather and I could feel my eyes wanting to water. I couldn't say anything. I just looked at him. He couldn't be saying what he was saying.

"I'll take care of him. He can eat part of my food. I won't eat anymore than usual. He won't cost anything to you. I'll pay for everything."

"Tim, it's not that. Too many farmers are losing their farm animals to coyotes. They can wipe out entire sheep herds within a year. If they knew we were raising one, I would probably lose all their business. We have to get rid of it. I'll take it."

I couldn't believe this was happening. Papaw reached down to pick it up. "No, Papaw! No!" The tears fell down my cheeks as I grabbed the pup and pulled it tight against my chest.

"I'm sorry, but I have to."

I felt like I hated my grandfather all of a sudden. My emotions were taking over my thoughts. I wanted this pup more than anything I had ever wanted. I had saved it. It counted on me to survive. I couldn't let Papaw, Robert or anyone else take and kill it. I rolled away from Papaw's hand and jumped up and ran toward the pond. I stopped and looked at my grandfather and said through my tears, "We don't even know if it is a coyote pup. You can't just kill it."

"Tim, come here," Papaw ordered.

"I can't."

Mamaw hurried out the back door. I looked at her, turned, and ran up the lane to the lake and kept running around the east side. This was the first time I had ever outright disobeyed my grandparents. It felt awful.

I slowed down and walked to the bridge where I had seen the two coyotes. I walked off the trail and made my way to the spot that the coyotes were sitting last summer. I sat on the rock under the cliff that overhung the small inlet of the lake. The pup began crying. I took the bottle from my pocket and it was still half full. When I held the nipple in front of him he quickly began to suckle it. He learned quickly. I thought it was a good sign. I wondered what I should do. I had run away from my papaw and disobeyed him. He could send me home or ground me for a while. I didn't know what to do next. I could find a place to hide the pup. I could come everyday to feed it, but I figured it would be too dangerous for such a small puppy.

I could see if James Ernest could keep it. But I didn't think his mom would let him have a dog. I actually didn't know what I would do with it. Papaw had never let a dog in the house. I would have to keep it outside. After the summer was over I knew I wouldn't be able to take it home to Ohio.

All I knew was that I couldn't let him die. He finished the bottle and tried to climb up into my lap. I helped him and he settled into my lap and closed his eyes.

The bad thing was, I understood Papaw's thinking, and I knew he was right about the coyotes being dangerous to the livestock. But it seemed to me that everything should have a place to live. The coyotes were here before we were. I didn't feel like we should kill them because they were doing what came naturally. The Indians had drawn pictures of them on the cave walls. They had always lived here. It still came down to the fact that we weren't sure it was a coyote.

Time passed as I sat there while the pup slept. I wasn't sure how long I had been there. I heard someone walking up the trail. I picked up the pup and laid flat on the ground. I heard my name called. "Timmy! Timmy! Where are you?" It was Susie's voice. I heard another voice on the other side of the lake calling my name.

When Susie got closer I called out, "I'm here."

"Where?"

"Come to the bridge and you'll see me."

Susie came into view and walked onto the bridge and I said, "I'm up here."

"Is it okay if I tell James Ernest where you are?" she asked.

"Sure it is." She then yelled across the lake and motioned for him to come over.

"How do I get up there?"

"Come across the bridge and there a small path coming up here. You'll see it." It was so good to see Susie. She didn't seem mad at me. She hurried up to where I was.

She soon saw the puppy next to me and said, "It's so cute. Can I hold it?"

I handed the pup to her and she held it like a mother would a baby. "Your papaw sent us to look for you. He and your mamaw are worried about where you went."

"Papaw and Robert want to kill it because it might be a coyote. I couldn't let them, so I left."

"Everyone is talking about it at the store. I would have done the same thing."

"Who is everyone?" I asked.

"Robert and his family, Homer and Ruby and our family are all there. They called everyone together for an announcement. But they don't want to make it until you're there also. Your grandparents want you to come back. Martin said we all would discuss the pup. Dad told them that you had a good head on your shoulders and that you wouldn't do anything that was wrong without strong feelings. So they agreed to listen to your plan for the pup."

"But I don't really have a plan. I just know that for some reason I found him before he died, and I can't let them kill him." James Ernest ran onto the bridge and I yelled at him as he was running on across, "James Ernest, we're up here."

He knew the way up. I'm sure he had been up there many times before. He was beside us before we could say another word. "Wow! Look at him."

Susie handed the pup to him and he held it out in front of him and looked into his face. He then stated very surely, "He's not full-blooded coyote."

"How do you know that?" I asked.

James Ernest explained, "I've seen full-blooded coyote pups. He's probably around three to four weeks old. A coyote pup's ears flop down until he's older and then they stand straight up. This puppy's ears will never stand straight up like a coyote. They're too big." I looked at James Ernest. He amazed me every time I was with him. I wanted to hug him.

"Will you tell Papaw that?"

"Sure, but he may not believe me."

"It couldn't hurt though," Susie said.

"Before we go, he may need to pee. He just drank a whole

bottle of milk." I put him down on the ground and said, "Go pee-pee." He smelled around and then leaned forward a little and peed. "Good boy. What a good puppy?"

Susie said, "You've already trained him."

"Yeah, right," I said as everyone laughed.

We took turns carrying the pup to the house. He kept looking for me when the other two were holding him. The twins were in the backyard when we came walking off the dam and we could here them yelling into the house that we were coming. Mamaw came out of the backdoor when we arrived. She had put a large cardboard box on the back porch and placed a couple of old towels inside it. She said that I could put the puppy in the box for now and for me to come get something to eat.

Thelma and Delma had gathered around the box and were looking at the pup.

"It probably has rabies or fleas," Delma said.

"I'm sure it has fleas and now Timmy has fleas," Thelma said.

"Timmy already had fleas. I'm sure he gave them to the puppy," Delma said.

"He probably gave the puppy rabies also," Thelma echoed.

I ignored them except to say, "Fleas can jump around five feet." They quickly moved away from the box as I walked into the kitchen. I ate my dinner fast. I knew that everyone was waiting for me. Robert and Janice's daughter, Tammy, was there and their son, Dana, was there with his pretty girlfriend, Idell. I walked out into the backyard where everyone had gathered while I ate. Everyone had been looking at the pup and talking about the pup.

"We have an announcement to make and Dana wanted to tell everyone in person. Dana, it's all yours," Janice said.

Dana's face turned red and Idell stood next to him and he said, "I'm proud to announce that Idell and I are engaged to be married." Everyone started clapping and hollering at the same time. Janice had tears in her eyes. We all started asking questions. Dana held up his hands and said, "Let us answer all the questions."

Idell began, "He asked me to marry him Wednesday night and I said I'd have to think about it," and then she laughed. "Not really. Of course I said yes right away."

"We've set a date of Saturday, August 27, this summer," Dana said. Everyone clapped and congratulated them and then we all had dessert as they talked about their engagement. Mamaw had fixed my favorite cherry dumplings.

After everyone ate, Papaw said, "I think we should have a discussion about the pup. I would like everyone's opinion." Papaw then restated his and Robert's concerns. Homer sat next to Uncle Morton and loudly repeated everything to him. Papaw then said, "Does anyone have anything to add in favor of getting rid of the pup before we let Tim state his reasoning." No one said anything.

Papaw motioned for me. I stood and picked up the pup from the box and held him high for everyone to see clearly. I began. I told how I had gone hiking to a spot I had never been before. I described how I heard the whimpering and found the pup abandoned.

"I really feel it was meant for me to find the puppy. And if it was meant for me to find it, then it couldn't be meant for us to kill it. It could have died where it was."

I then asked James Ernest to tell what he knew. He told them what a coyote pup looked like. He then said, "It could be part coyote, but definitely not full-blooded."

Susie stood and said, "Why not take it to the vet and see what he says about it? He should be able to tell if it's a coyote or not. If it is, then there are wildlife places and zoos that would take him. You don't have to kill him."

Brenda, Susie oldest sister, was sitting in the back with the twins. She stood and said, "I agree with Susie. You can't just kill it."

Papaw then said, "Even if it's not a coyote. Your mom won't let you take it home when the summer is up. What will happen to it?"

Delma stood and said, "We'll take it."

Thelma looked up at her in bewilderment and stood and said, "We would take it."

Susie said, "We need a dog at the farm."

Tammy stood and said, "Daddy, you can't kill a puppy. We could take it."

Ruby then said, "I'll take it, before I watch that dog killed."

Uncle Morton said, "Maybe it could be a seeing-eye dog for me?"

"That's just what you need, a coyote for a seeing-eye dog," Homer said, shaking his head. "We would end up in *Ripley's Believe It or Not*."

"Okay! I give up. Your arguments are good. Monday morning, Tim and I will take the pup to Dr. Green and see what he says. We'll get him shots and see if Doc thinks he's going to make it." Everyone cheered. I even saw Robert clapping. "Also

Tim, you're grounded tomorrow for disobeying today," Papaw added

I smiled and said, "Yes sir."

Mamaw said, "You kids take the pup to the creek with some shampoo and give it a bath."

Susie and I walked toward the creek and Delma and Thelma tagged along. James Ernest wanted to stay and eat another dessert. Susie wanted to carry the pup.

I said, "Thanks for taking up for the pup. I apologize for everything. Please forgive me."

"You're forgiven," Susie said. I wasn't sure what I apologized about, but I just wanted Susie to not be mad at me anymore.

"You can't kill a puppy just because he might be part coyote," Susie reasoned.

"Yeah, but he might be a killer coyote," Delma said.

"I think he is a killer coyote," Thelma added.

"Maybe he'll kill Timmy and eat him," Delma suggested.

Thelma seriously said, "We can only hope."

"You girls should be ashamed of yourselves," Susie scolded.

"Maybe we should, but we're not," Delma told her.

Thelma nodded her head in agreement as I said, "I think I'll train him to attack little girls." Susie and I laughed.

By then we were at the creek and Susie placed him in a shallow section of the creek and began wetting him down. The twins stood on the bank and watched and made snide remarks as I poured shampoo on his back and began rubbing him down. The pup bent down and slurped a drink of water. I washed every bit of him and made sure to suds him up again, and Susie scrubbed him down. I carried him out into deeper water and rinsed him off. He seemed to enjoy the water and it somehow made him livelier.

I placed him on the bank and the twins stood there laughing at him.

"He looks like a drowned rat," Delma teased.

"Even uglier," Thelma added.

The pup ran right in between the twins. The girls bent down to tease him again, and he began shaking the water off and it flew all over the twins.

"Gross," Delma yelled.

They both backed up hurriedly in opposite directions and Delma fell backwards. The pup thought she was playing and he ran to her and began climbing on her. She started screaming and the pup excitedly jumped on her more.

"The coyote is attacking Delma," Thelma screamed.

Susie and I laughed and laughed at the sight. I went over and picked the pup up and Delma rose and the two of them ran toward the store screaming, "That dog is a monster! It could have killed me! Wait until we tell mom. No way are we keeping it!"

Mamaw had given me an old towel to dry him off, and I began rubbing him down.

"You taught those girls a lesson for calling you a rat," I said to the pup.

"What are you going to name him?" Susie asked.

"I don't know."

"You found him in a den. How about Denny?"

"No. I don't think I like that name. The den was under a large rock. I could name him Rocky."

Susie thought for a few seconds as I was finished drying the pup off when she smiled and said, "I got one I like."

"What?"

"Since he might be part coyote, how about naming him Coty?"

I knew that would be his name as soon as I heard it. I picked up the shampoo, and Susie and I turned to walk back to the store. I looked back at the pup and he stood there looking at us like, 'Who's picking me up?' I said, "Come on, Coty. You have to start walking on your own." He quickly began running toward us. It looked like he had a smile on his face.

We walked around the house and Coty started running up to everyone. He looked so much fluffier and cuter after his bath. Everyone wanted to pet him and play with him. The twins kept telling people to watch themselves because he was a killer coyote. Coty's name was a hit with everyone, and everyone seemed to really like him except Leo. Leo sniffed him and went immediately to his doghouse. Even Papaw and Robert were seen petting him and smiling. Coty was a happy puppy. I was a happy kid.

It had been a great day. I was anxious to take Coty to the vet. I went to bed as soon as everyone left. Papaw and Mamaw said Coty could sleep in his cardboard box next to my bed.

Dr. Green's office was a mile outside of West Liberty on a small farm. Susie went with us. We walked into the office and there was only one other person there. A large lady sat in the corner holding a small pig. Papaw and I found chairs to sit while Susie had to go see the pig. Susie looked down at the pig and screamed. She tried to cover her mouth and muffle the sound, but everyone in the building could hear her. The piglet had three eyes. Susie's screaming made Coty start barking and soon he began to howl. The pig squealed and slipped out of the woman's lap and began running and sliding on the linoleum floor. Coty jumped off my lap before I could get a good hold on him and started chasing the piglet all over the room.

It was quite a sight seeing the puppy and the piglet sliding around the floor. The lady jumped up and started chasing her pig trying to get to it before Coty got it. Coty was just having fun. He wanted to play with the pig, I hoped. The lady bent down to pick up the pig and lost her balance and slid head first between Papaw's legs and wedged her body between the legs of Papaw's plastic white chair.

The secretary ran around the counter to help Papaw as he got up. They both tried to pull the chair off the lady. Everyone forgot about Coty and the pig. We were watching the sight of two adults trying to pull a fat lady out from between the legs of a chair. She screamed and yelled, even more, at the top of her lungs. We looked down to see Coty chewing on her large huge butt. Papaw said, "I'll be, it looks like Coty is eating two big ham-hocks." We all laughed, and Coty just chewed and howled and chewed. When we looked around for the piglet, all we saw were bones scattered in the corner.

9 TWO PIECE

MONDAY, JUNE 20

The morning came early and I woke up in a sweat. What a nightmare—Coty eating a piglet and attacking a woman at the vet's office. I hoped the dream wasn't a sign of things to come. I looked down to find Coty. He was stirring in his box by the bed, wanting out. I had gotten up in the middle of the night to feed him milk from the bottle and let him out to pee. Coty was excited to get me up and get on with his life. It was exciting for me to see him wanting to be with me.

I had spent all day Saturday doing chores and helping in the store since I was grounded. Coty had slept in his box and followed me around out in the yard. I let him out on the front porch and he jumped all over Leo. Leo barely woke up and when he did he took his big paw and knocked Coty away. This made Coty feel he had a playmate and he jumped on him again. Leo had had enough and he got up and left.

Sunday was church Sunday. Pastor Black was the pastor of two churches, so he alternated holding services every other week. He made an announcement that stunned everyone. He said that he felt he couldn't do the Lord's will serving two churches and that he was going to give up the Oak Hills Church. He would begin having services every Sunday at his other church and that the congregation should start interviewing for a new pastor.

Everyone was shocked, but a lot of members were excited about a new start for the church.

Randy and Purty and James Ernest spent the afternoon at the store with me playing Wiffleball. Coty ran after the ball when we hit it. His small awkward legs wore out quickly and he just laid in the grass and watched us. The Wolf Pack loved Coty and it was voted unanimously to make him the club mascot and honorary member since he was a boy.

Susie came back down to visit Sunday evening with her family. Everything seemed to be back to normal between us, which made me happy. As much fun as it was to be with the Wolf Pack, I enjoyed being with Susie more. I would never tell the guys that though. I told Susie about the nightmare and we laughed about it.

Susie said, "I hope that doesn't come true."

"Me too," I said.

Susie asked Papaw, "Can I go with you tomorrow when you take Coty to the veterinarian." Papaw of course said yes. I explained to Papaw how Susie wanted to be a vet and that she loved going to see Dr. Green and see what he was doing with all the animals.

Papaw called at nine o'clock to see when Dr. Green could see Coty. He was told to come in anytime before noon. They weren't very busy. Papaw and I and Coty drove up to Clayton's farm to pick up Susie at ten and headed to West Liberty. Coty was getting stronger every day. Susie and I took turns holding Coty while the truck rambled along Licking Creek to town. I had brought a bottle of milk if he got hungry. Susie fed him. After he drank the milk he wanted to chew on the nipple of the bottle.

Dr. Green's office was a mile outside of West Liberty on a small farm. His office was attached to the farmhouse where he lived. He was a tall thin older gentleman with a friendly smile, graying hair, and wire-rimmed glasses that sat awry on his face. We walked into the office and there was only one other person there. It wasn't a large lady holding a small pig. It was a man with a rooster. I held on to Coty real tight. No way was I going to let him loose. After the Doc saw the rooster he came out to greet Papaw.

"Hello, Doc. Good to see you," Papaw said.

"Well, there's Susie. How have you been?"

"Great, I'm tagging along to see all the animals." Susie then introduced me to Dr. Green.

"This here is Coty. I found him Friday," I explained.

"Let's go back and take a look at him. He's a good looking puppy," Dr. Green said. He took the puppy and sat him on a table and began checking him. He talked to Coty and played with him and watched different things about him. He looked in his ears and checked his heartbeat and then looked in his eyes.

"We are worried that he might be a coyote pup or at least part coyote," Papaw finally said.

"Where did you find him?" Dr. Green asked.

I explained where and how I had found him. I told him how I was feeding him. I told him how much Coty had improved in the three days.

"Was that Coty yapping at the rooster?" he asked.

I answered, "Yes." I then told Dr. Green and Papaw about the dream. "I was glad there was a rooster in the waiting room instead of a three-eyed pig."

"Sometimes you get a freak in nature. I once saw a calf born with two heads and a chicken with six legs."

"Everyone would get a chicken leg when they fried it up," Papaw said. Everyone laughed.

"Those really happened?" I asked.

"I was teasing about the chicken, but the calf was true. It died at birth," Dr. Green answered.

"Do you think the pup is a coyote?" Papaw asked after the Doc got done checking Coty.

I held my breath. I wasn't sure what they would do with Coty if he was. I looked at Susie. She seemed just as concerned. Coty yapping at the rooster didn't help.

"No. He could be part, but not even half. My guess is he could be a quarter coyote. Coyotes mate for life, unless one is killed or dies. Then they might mate with a domestic dog. The half-breeds are shunned by the full breeds and won't mate with them. So I think what happened was a half breed female mated with another domestic dog and we have Coty. Since the pack won't readily accept the pups, my guess is they were abandoned when the pack wanted to move on. You happened to be in the right place at the right time to save this one."

"What other breeds do you think he might be?" Papaw asked.

Dr. Green thought for a moment and said, "I think he's got some collie and maybe some Shepherd. It's hard to tell. But I think he's going to be a fine dog and a good pet." My face lit up and my smile must have stretched across the room. Susie was jumping up and down clapping.

But Papaw still asked, "By being part coyote, would he ever revert back to being dangerous to us or livestock."

"I understand your concern. Most farmers hate coyotes and would love to wipe them off the earth. I can't guarantee that he won't chase a chicken, but most domestic dogs will do that. Remember, all dogs came from what God created and the two that were saved on the Ark. I don't think you'll have any problems if you raise Coty with love."

Papaw looked at me and said, "Okay, you can keep him."

Susie and I both ran over and hugged Papaw. Susie gave Dr. Green a hug and I shook his hand and thanked him. Dr. Green gave Coty his shots and some pills he would need to take to make sure he wouldn't get worms. He then said we should keep feeding him milk for another week and we could try giving Coty some soft dog food also. He would be able to eat solid food within a couple of weeks.

The doctor thanked me for saving Coty and then asked if we would like to see the other animals. Susie would have killed us if we had said no. We walked outside to some other buildings, and I couldn't believe all the different animals he had. He said people brought hurt wild animals to him all the time, and he would cure them and set them free if they were able. He had a raccoon, a rabbit, a squirrel, and two deer. A Red-Tailed Hawk stood on a large limb in one large cage. He said its wing was healing and he hoped it would be okay soon. He had all kinds of dogs and cats and even horses and cows in his barn. He had a large fenced area behind the barn. He said we would be especially interested in what was inside it. We stood there looking, but couldn't see anything. Dr. Green whistled and soon a coyote crept out from behind a rock. Her right front leg was missing.

"See how her tail is tucked down between her legs. That's a sure sign of a coyote. Coty keeps his tail up. A family ran over this one and brought it to me. I had to remove her leg. She'll never be released, but she's okay here."

She was beautiful. Her coat was grayish-brown. She had yellow eyes, a narrow muzzle with a black nose, tall triangular ears and a long bushy tail. Coty walked up to the fence and looked at her and whimpered.

We soon said our goodbyes and Papaw drove back into town. Papaw dropped us off at the General store and he went to the bank. Papaw said that I should pick out a collar and a lease for Coty. Mr. Cobb, the store owner, saw us coming and met us at the door. I introduced Susie and Coty and asked if Coty could come inside to try on some collars. Mr. Cobb didn't mind at all. He even held Coty while Susie and I looked at the selection of collars.

We picked out a brown leather collar and a ten-foot leash. Susie and I then went over to the dog food section and found some canned dog food for puppies. Susie said she had some money and wanted to buy Coty some soft dog treats.

"We can use them to teach Coty some tricks. I've read how to do it in some of the animal books I get from the library," she explained.

"Okay."

Papaw had arrived and was talking to Mr. Cobb. I looked toward them and saw Papaw holding Coty and petting him.

Papaw paid for the things we had picked out. He even said he would pay for the treats that Susie had gotten. He liked the collar.

"Would we have time to run by the library for a few minutes? I'd like to find some books on dogs and coyotes," I asked. I hadn't thought much of the library since last summer. The last time I had been in it was when the Natalie Robbins Children's Library Section was opened with the money from Mrs. Robbins' estate. At the same time I was presented with a check for one hundred dollars for the capture of the Tattoo Man. I placed the collar around Coty's neck. He didn't seem to mind it.

Papaw parked in front, and Susie and I ran in while Papaw walked Coty with the new leash. It looked kind of funny.

I checked out a couple of books with Susie's library card, and she found two books she wanted to read. We walked over to the children's section just to see Mrs. Robbins' name on the wall. Then we hurried out to find Papaw talking to some men in front of the barber shop which was just down the block.

On the way back to the house I asked Susie if she could stay the afternoon and go swimming. She said she would like to but needed to go home and get her swimming suit and ask her mom. Papaw drove her up to the farm to ask. Monie said yes.

When we got back to the store, we fed Coty some milk and he quickly went to sleep. Mamaw fixed us sandwiches for lunch and we ate. Then I changed into my swimming trunks and we headed to the swimming hole. Coty walked by my side, and when he acted tired we carried him. He slept near the water while we swam. We were there nearly a half hour when we heard voices.

We looked down the trail and saw the guys heading toward us. Randy and Purty were leading and James Ernest was walking with someone behind them. When they got closer I realized that Sadie was with them.

As they got within earshot Purty said, "You guys should have called us. We like to swim. Quit hogging the pool." He kicked off his shoes and threw off his shirt and did a big belly flop right between us, making a gigantic splash. Everyone laughed.

Randy soon followed him into the swimming hole. James Ernest said hello and sat down to pet Coty, who had awakened in all the commotion.

Sadie walked over to the ledge and looked at Susie and me and said, "Hi, Susie. How are you?"

"I'm great. How are you?" Susie replied back.

Sadie didn't answer her. She looked at me and said, "Hello, Timmy. I've missed you since the last time we went for our walk."

"Hi." She made it sound like we always went for walks.

Sadie began taking off her shorts and top. She slowly removed her top revealing the fact that she had on a two piece. As she slid her shorts off, I turned and started splashing Purty. Next thing I knew Sadie jumped in right next to me. She grabbed me around the shoulders and tried to dunk me. Coty started barking and he jumped in and started swimming toward me. Sadie was still hanging on to me from behind, and I couldn't get to Coty. Susie swam over and grabbed him before he could tire out and drown.

I thought I could see the water boiling around Susie. I finally got Sadie off my back and made it over to Susie. Susie placed Coty back on the rock where he had been sleeping. She turned and stared at me. I looked at her and put my palms up trying to motion that I didn't have anything to do with Sadie being here. I certainly didn't tell her to jump on my back.

James Ernest swam over and said that Randy had called the store looking for me and that Mamaw had told him that we had just left to go swimming. "So we all decided to meet you guys here. Sadie wanted to come along since Susie was here. We couldn't very well say no."

Susie seemed to be happier after James Ernest explained it. We all played games and did dives off the banks and judged them. Purty did nothing but belly flops, but he was good at them and he won. Ten minutes after the diving competition I saw Purty's trunks laying on the bank.

"Todd, put your pants back on," I yelled.

Purty pleaded, "Come on, let's go skinny dipping." Susie turned her head away from Purty and everyone yelled no. He put them back on despite his many protests.

"I will if everyone else will," Sadie suddenly spoke up.

Purty yelled yes and pulled his pants off in a flash and threw them back onto the bank.

Randy said no to both of them. I said no, and Susie didn't say anything. She kept her head turned away from the pool.

Randy yelled, "Purty, put your pants back on and leave them on. There are girls here. Show some respect."

"Gosh, okay."

Susie and I got out of the swimming hole and sat on our towels with Coty in the middle. Coty wanted to play. So we began rubbing his belly and twisting him all around. Sadie got out of the water and walked over and sat down between us, kind of making a triangle with Coty in the middle.

"Susie, do you like my bathing suit. It's the newest style." She didn't wait for an answer as she began talking about how cute she thought James Ernest was. "He's very sweet also. I think he likes me too. He's always looking at me with those big eyes of his."

"I never noticed him having big eyes," I said.

"He sure does. Doesn't he Susan? His eyes are very dreamy," Sadie continued.

I didn't even know what dreamy eyes meant.

"Does that mean he looks sleepy?" I asked.

Sadie laughed and touched my arm and said, "Timmy, you are so funny. I just love you." She kept her hand on my arm and I quickly got up and walked to the other side of the swimming hole. Coty followed me and I motioned for James Ernest to swim over to me.

"What's up?" he asked.

"Apparently Sadie has a thing for you. Do you like her?"

"Did she send you over to ask me?"

"No. I just had to get away. Do you?"

"I think she's cute. I'm still a little scared of her. I guess she's okay, but I don't really know her very well. What do you think?"

I hesitated for a moment trying to find the right words of how I felt about her. I looked at Susie and Sadie sitting together looking bored. Neither of them was talking to the other. I looked at James Ernest and said, "I think she's trouble, but you should like her if you want to."

We all got back in the pool because Purty was begging for everyone to play underwater tag. We all had fun and it wore everyone out. We all left at the same time. Sadie walked with James Ernest. Susie and I walked with Randy and Purty. Everyone went on home except for Susie; she stayed to eat dinner with us. We watched television for a while and played with Coty. We taught him to sit; he loved the small bits of soft treats.

Around eight o'clock, Clayton came to pick up Susie, and he brought Uncle Morton back with him. We told them all about what the vet had said, and they seemed pleased. I said goodbye to Susie, and we promised to spend another afternoon together soon. I went out back to put the tent up before it got dark. Coty and I slept in the tent together. He curled up in a little ball and slept right against me.

10 THE TURKEY BASTER

The weather turned hot, therefore the Wiffleball league was suspended until it cooled off a little. I spent my days working in the store and helping Papaw build some new benches around the pay lake in the mornings while it was still under eighty-five degrees. Coty was growing like a weed. He was eating almost anything now. I enjoyed almost everything about him except for the fact that his sharp little teeth chewed on me every chance he got. Papaw said he was teething and it would last for a while.

I gave him sticks and large bones and anything else I could find to keep him from chewing me. His teeth were as sharp as pin pricks. My hands and lower arms had teeth marks all over them. James Ernest would come to the house some afternoons and we would play cards and board games.

Papaw got a call last night telling him the church was having a special meeting with other men of the church to interview a candidate for pastor of the church. The candidate had been recommended by the church headquarters. The meeting was going to be tonight. Papaw told us he was surprised anyone wanted to be the pastor of such a small church for hardly any pay. How could a pastor support a family? He thought as long as the guy was breathing they would vote for him, and maybe even if he wasn't.

Uncle Morton was sitting on the front porch. It was mid-morning. I was sitting in a rocker keeping him company and watching Coty chew on Leo. Leo took one of his big paws and knocked Coty down and held him down.

"That will teach you," I said.

An old blue Buick pulled into the parking lot and an elderly gray-haired thin lady opened the door and got out. I had seen her once before, but it had been a couple of years, I thought.

She looked up at us. "Good morning. Hi there, Morton," she said. Morton didn't acknowledge her since he didn't hear her. She looked at him puzzled and asked, "Are you Timmy?"

"Yes, ma'am."

"I remember when you were born. I haven't seen you for a while now. I wouldn't ever forget a handsome boy like you."

I blushed. "Thank you. How do you know me?"

"I delivered you when you were born. I was the midwife in these parts for years. I helped birth almost everyone around here. Plus, I helped heal most people with whatever ailed them."

"Are you a doctor?"

She laughed. She had a very appealing laugh. Almost like you would think birds would laugh if they could. She answered, "No. Not with a license if that's what you mean. But I'll tell you a secret, I'm smarter than most of them. Don't tell them I said so. I might need their help some day. Thank God I haven't so far, knock on wood." She laughed her bird laugh and knocked on one of the wooden posts that held the porch up.

Papaw came through the door and said, "I thought I heard a familiar voice out here." He gave her a hug in greeting. "How are you doing Geraldine? What brings you to these parts of the woods?"

"What's left of our family is having a reunion down at the Natural Bridge Park tomorrow and I'm passing through on my way. I couldn't pass by without saying hello."

"We're glad you did. Come in. Corie will be so happy to see you."

Geraldine and Papaw went in and Uncle Morton suddenly said, "Who's there?"

"Geraldine. She helped when I was born," I yelled into his ear.

"I've got to see her. Help me into the house to where she is."

We slowly made our way into the kitchen where Mamaw and Geraldine were both laughing and talking at the same time. "Mamaw, she helped when I was born," I said.

"I remember. She was the first person to ever touch you," Mamaw said.

"She was the first person to see you naked also," Papaw said. Everyone laughed and I said, "Too much information for me."

Uncle Morton sat down at the table. "Good to see you, Geraldine," he said.

"You're still giving us the same old jokes I see," Geraldine joked.

Uncle Morton didn't say anything. "He can't hear you. He's going deaf," I spoke up.

"That's why he didn't say anything to me out on the porch. What's causing it?" she asked.

"I need your help," Uncle Morton said. "I can't hear anything."

Papaw told Uncle Morton that they were talking about it.

Mamaw told Geraldine about the numbness and the loss of hearing.

Geraldine walked over to Uncle Morton and bent down and yelled, "I'm going to look you over."

"I knew you would end up flirting with me again," Uncle Morton said and laughed.

"You old fool. You wish someone would flirt with you."

"You're always right, Geraldine."

Geraldine took hold of his arm and had Papaw yell her questions to Uncle Morton. She wanted to know exactly what had numbness and where the tingling was. She then turned and went out to her car and came back with an old wooden box that looked like a carpenter's box. She placed it on the sink counter and opened it. I walked over and looked inside. There were all kinds of tools and instruments. I recognized almost nothing except for a stethoscope.

She took out a pair of needle-nose pliers and asked if we had a flashlight. I ran to my bedroom and got mine out of the nightstand drawer. I wondered what in the world she was going to do. I was totally fascinated. Coty was at the back door whining for me. I ignored him. I was too interested in what Geraldine was going to do to Uncle Morton.

She told Papaw to tell Morton to sit very still. She took the pliers and stuck them into Morton's right ear and spread it apart. She asked for the flashlight and I handed it to her. She shined the light into his ear and looked inside as close as she could.

"Do you have a turkey baster?" she asked Mamaw.

Mamaw looked at her with a puzzled frown and answered, "Yes. I'll get it."

"We'll need to heat some water."

She told Uncle Morton that she thought she might have an idea what might be wrong. When the water was warm enough she took the turkey baster and sucked out some of the water and squirted it into Uncle Morton's ear. She then sucked the water back out of his ear. She kept doing it repeatedly. She squeezed the used water into an empty can that Mamaw gave her. She then went to work on the other ear doing the same thing. After nearly a half-hour she put down the baster and sat in front of Uncle Morton. Uncle Morton began lifting his arm and smiling.

Geraldine in a whispered voice asked, "You still want me to flirt with you?"

"Anytime you want to will be fine with me," Uncle Morton said. A grin spread across his face.

We all started clapping and laughing and crying. Mamaw said, "Praise the Lord."

"All this noise is too much for my ears," Uncle Morton said as he laughed with tears flowing down his cheeks. I had tears. All I could do was stand and clap and bounce around in circles. I couldn't believe it.

After the excitement died down, Geraldine said, "Morton, I was afraid when I squirted the water in your right ear that it would just come out the left." We all laughed again. She said she had taken out the ear wax that had built up over the many years. She explained that some people had more than others and that just cleaning your ears didn't really help stop the wax that built up deep down inside.

Geraldine emptied the water and showed us the clumps of earwax that she was able to soften with the hot water and then suck out with the baster. It was unbelievable how much was taken out.

"I thought it would help your hearing."

"But did you know that all the numbness and tingling would go away," Uncle Morton asked.

We all looked at Uncle Morton. Geraldine looked as surprised as anything. She finally managed to say, "Are you telling me that all the numbness went away?"

"I sure am."

"The tingling too," Papaw said.

"I'm back to normal." Mamaw had to sit down. Everyone was just stunned.

"Geraldine, how is that possible?" Papaw finally spoke.

Geraldine shrugged her shoulders and said, "Beats me. The body is an amazing thing. God truly outdid Himself when he created man and woman. Some things affect other things. That's the only way I can explain it."

Uncle Morton laughed and asked, "Can you do anything about this broken toe and eyesight?"

"Your broken toe will heal itself and you're better off blind. If you could see me, my beauty would overwhelm you." She laughed and gave Uncle Morton a big kiss on his cheek.

Mamaw asked, "Can you stay for a while. Everyone would like to see you."

She said she could stay for a couple of hours. Mamaw headed for the phone. Uncle Morton heard her dialing the rotary phone and asked her not to tell them what had happened. "Let's surprise them." Mamaw called Robert and Janice, Homer and Ruby and the Perry's and told them they needed to come as soon as possible.

"Nothing bad has happened, but you need to come." Mamaw told them.

Robert picked up Homer and Ruby and they were the first to arrive. "What's this all about?" they asked as they entered the front door. They saw Geraldine and hugs began. Everyone suspected that Geraldine was the surprise and never thought about Uncle Morton. As everyone started catching up with Geraldine's life, Clayton and Monie and the girls walked in.

Geraldine had helped in the birth of all of Monie's girls.

"Weren't Thelma and I the cutest babies you ever laid eyes on?" Delma asked Geraldine.

"We were, weren't we?" Thelma baited.

Geraldine laughed. "Actually, you were about the home-liest babies I ever saw. You both were wrinkled and hairless. You looked like baby pigs when they're born," she answered the twins.

Delma and Thelma stood there with their hands on their hips and shocked looks on their faces. "Timmy was one of the prettiest babies I ever seen."

This left the twins with the most soured faces a person had ever seen. I laughed at them. "But look how cute you two turned out. You can't tell what a person is going to look like at birth," Geraldine then said.

Their faces suddenly lit up and Delma said, "You're right, because look how ugly Timmy is now."

"He looks like the pig now," Thelma added.

Uncle Morton had been sitting quietly at the table not reacting to any of the conversation when he finally said, "I can even see that Timmy doesn't look like a pig, girls."

The twins were thinking of something to say when Susie,

surprising everyone, turned to Uncle Morton and asked, "You could hear that?"

Everyone then realized that Uncle Morton could hear the twins. "Yes. I heard everything. Geraldine has healed me," Uncle Morton answered.

Questions started flying around the kitchen and there was laughter and clapping and the praising of God and Geraldine. Coty began howling at the back door. It was a very happy place. Morton showed them how all the numbness and tingling was gone and he demonstrated how he again could hear a pin drop. He had me take Susie into the living room and whisper something into her ear. He then told everyone that I had whispered, "I'm glad I got to keep Coty."

Everyone clapped again and then Papaw showed everyone the nuggets of earwax that had been removed from Uncle Morton's ears. The twins ran around the house yelling, "Gross, gross. That is so gross." We even heard Delma say, "Didn't he ever clean his ears with a Q-tip."

"Of course he didn't," Thelma agreed.

"Well, this was worth being pulled from the fields to see. I'm very happy for you Morton," Clayton finally said.

"Thank you. It was truly awful not being to hear all my family and friends that I love. I missed it a lot more than not seeing you. I missed hearing the laughter. I even missed hearing the twins—kind of."

"How rude! How very rude," the twins said.

Everyone stayed until Geraldine had to leave. Then everyone began leaving. Uncle Morton wanted to go home. I helped him pack all his things and Papaw took him home. Uncle Morton told me he wanted to fish with me soon, and I agreed that it would be fun.

11 BARTHOLOMEW WALKER WHITE

Mom called and talked to me for a while. I told her how Coty was growing and how much I loved him. I talked to Janie for a minute. Mom said that Dad hadn't been feeling so well lately. She said everything else was fine. She said they were thinking about trying to come down for the Fourth of July.

I was very happy that they might be coming. I wondered what was wrong with Dad. Mamaw talked to Mom after I was finished. Mamaw seemed very concerned with whatever Mom was telling her. I wondered if they were discussing Dad not feeling well. I also wondered if they would want me to go back home with them if Dad was still sick. I might be able to help in some way.

There was a special church service this morning to meet the preacher that might take the place of Pastor Black, even though this was the Sunday that we didn't have service. Mamaw said that we would have church service every Sunday if the church found a full time preacher. That didn't sound very good to me. Papaw said that the meeting with the candidate went well and that we would probably like him. Papaw said he was pretty young to be a pastor, he was breathing though.

Papaw put out a sign on the front door telling people we were at church. It said fishermen could pay later and if they needed bait to get it out of the refrigerator on the back porch. Papaw thought he should be there to hear the young preacher. The women had spread the word around the county to everyone that went to church and some that didn't, inviting all of them to come.

It did seem like there was an excitement in the air as we parked in the church lot. The lot was crowded and men were entering the building instead of taking their usual spot on the tailgates in the parking lot. All of the church windows were open and a nice breeze blew across the congregation as they whispered and waited for the young pastor to be brought in. Susie and her family came and sat with us. James Ernest was there with his mom, and sat behind us. I had never seen his mom anywhere other than the store. She didn't seem very social. It was good to see them there.

It was five minutes after the service time and everyone was just sitting and waiting. No sign of the preacher.

Suddenly the back door opened. The same door that James Ernest and I had snuck out of three weeks earlier. A young man with dark black wavy hair walked through the door. He wore a black pair of slacks and a blue short sleeve shirt with small white stripes in it. He didn't have a tie or suit jacket on. The congregation whispered and had quite a buzz going throughout the building as he walked up to the pulpit. Could this be the new pastor candidate? I thought there was no way.

"Hello, I'm Bartholomew Walker White. I'm twenty-nine years old. I'm not married, yet," he opened. The congregation chuckled. He continued, "I want to serve people who want to walk closely with God. I want to serve people who want to see their friends and family and enemies come to know Jesus as their Lord and Savior. I want to help serve the community by being there when the rough times come. When loved ones are buried and when loved ones are married. I want to baptize the new believers in the creek down by the Collins' grocery.

"I want to eat the food that you ladies prepare for church picnics. I want to be invited to your homes for dinner. Remember, I'm single, and not much of a cook." The pews filled with laughter. "I want to teach your kids to love and honor God, but to not be terrified of God. I want to teach them what Christ did for them on the cross. I want all of you to know how much Christ loves you no matter what you've done in the past. I want to worship God alongside you, with our lives. I want to be your new pastor."

Susie and I began clapping. I knew that we liked him. The clapping grew to include almost everyone.

Mr. White then said, "I know that Pastor Black always wore a suit in church and I see that most of you men have on suits, or at least ties. Aren't you hot? All the men can take off their ties and unbutton that top button around your neck. You can take off that jacket. How can someone be comfortable hearing God's word taught when you're uncomfortable to begin with? This is by no means any disrespect to Pastor Black. I guess you could say we're as different as black and white." Everyone laughed again.

Papaw stood up and took off his jacket and unclipped his tie and sat back down. Clayton followed and Homer stood and did the same. Soon, almost all the men had removed their ties or at least loosened them. Robert Easterling yelled out, "That sure does feel better, Pastor White."

"Amen," floated around the room.

"Let's sing "Amazing Grace" to begin the service. Please stand as we sing." He led the congregation in the hymn. You could tell that everyone sang a little softer because this man had a voice of the angels. It was strong, but soft and beautiful. What couldn't this man do?

He then preached a sermon about some men who brought their sick friend to hear Jesus preach. They couldn't get him in the doors so they took him up on the roof and lowered him through the roof to Jesus. He said we should take any effort to get someone to hear the Gospel of Jesus. The preacher was funny and serious and I actually enjoyed being there. Pastor Black always yelled at us and it would scare me. Mr. White was more like a good teacher.

The service ended when we sang another song and the preacher prayed. One of the men announced that all the men should meet this evening at six to vote on Mr. White as pastor. Everyone wanted to meet Mr. White after the service. While we waited in line I saw Miss Rebecca Simmons and her son Bobby Lee standing in line. I ran up to them and said, "Hello. I didn't know you two went to church."

"Hi, Timmy, of course we do. We're not heathens. We feel more like a part of the community now, and I got a call telling us about the special service, so we decided to come. I enjoyed the service." Rebecca was dressed in a light blue sundress. She was beautiful.

"I've been meaning to come up to visit, but I've been busy."

"You just come any time you want to. We would love that, wouldn't we Bobby Lee?"

"Bring your puppy. I heard you got a puppy," Bobby Lee said.

"Okay. I will. Bobby Lee, come with me. I want you to meet two people. Is that okay Miss Rebecca?"

"Sure, he needs to meet new friends."

I led Bobby Lee to Delma and Thelma, a mean trick to pull on a kid.

"I would like for you two to meet Bobby Lee. Bobby Lee, these are two of your neighbors, Delma and Thelma."

Bobby Lee started laughing and then he asked, "Is that really your names?"

Delma said, "Yes, they are great names you little squirt."

"Hey, I'm not a little squirt, you cootie head."

"Don't call my sister a name, Bobby *Flea*."

"Bobby *Flea* boy," Delma added.

Bobby Lee looked them in the eyes and said, "Is your mom's name Selma and your sister's are probably Wilma and Pilma?"

I hadn't planned on a full out fight, but I felt it was beginning to become one so I grabbed Bobby Lee by the arm and pulled him back to his mom. I heard Delma say, "What a rude little squirt. Where did he come from?"

"He probably squirted out from under a rock," Thelma said.

Bobby Lee turned his head back toward them. "I did not!" he yelled.

I got him back to his mom just before she introduced herself to Mr. White.

It wasn't long before we made it to Preacher White. Papaw introduced us.

"It's a pleasure to meet you Mrs. Collins. Timmy, I've heard a lot about you. You became very famous last summer. I'm honored to meet you."

"Thank you. I enjoyed the sermon about the friends today. I hope you become the pastor."

"Thank you. If the Lord wants me here, it'll happen," he explained.

"I think God talked to me last summer." I couldn't believe I said it. Why would I say that out of the blue? I figured he thought I was crazy.

He smiled at me and said, "I would love to sit down and have you tell me about that some time."

We walked out of the Church and I saw Uncle Morton standing at the bottom of the steps. I walked over to him and grabbed his arm and asked if I could help him to the car. "That would be nice of you, Timmy."

"I liked the preacher."

"I did too, a very nice young man. He sounded real good. What does he look like?"

I explained his looks and Uncle Morton said, "Every young woman in the state will start attending this church." He laughed and added, "Whatever it takes to get them to church is a good thing."

I dropped Uncle Morton off at Robert and Janice's car and looked for Susie. She was climbing into the back of the truck and I ran over to her and asked, "Do you want to go for a walk this afternoon after dinner?"

She asked Monie and I said I would be up later. I ran back to Papaw's green truck and jumped into the bed. I was excited for the afternoon. Spending time with Susie was always fun.

When we got home the phone was ringing. I ran to answer it. "Hello."

"Timmy, this is Susie."

"Hi."

"When you come up, bring your swimming trunks and we'll go swimming in the pond."

"Okay. Is it okay if Coty comes along?"

"Sure."

"See you later."

Mamaw was already in the kitchen beginning to cook dinner. Papaw asked me to watch the store while he went to the lake to collect any money that was owed him by the fishermen. I changed clothes quickly and went into the store. Two young men came into the store. They were picking out pop and snacks and were teasing each other about being really hungry. The taller guy had sandy colored hair and was haggard looking. The shorter one had dark shorter hair and a nice friendly smile.

"How come you guys are so hungry?" I asked.

"We've been on a hiking trip and we ran out of food. We just came off the trail."

"Where is this trail at?"

The shorter hiker explained, "It starts up Morgan Road where it crosses the creek north of that swinging bridge. It's easy to miss. It winds up the mountain to a community called Blaze and then circles back around. There's a long loop that takes around four days and a shorter loop that only that's two days. We took the four-day loop and ran out of food on the third day."

His friend said, "We didn't realize how hungry we would get hiking. We almost ate everything the first day."

I wondered if the trail to the cabin was the same one they talked about. "You don't have a map of the trail do you?" I asked them.

They laid all the stuff on the counter. I began adding it up, thinking they had ignored my question. They paid for the food and drinks and as they were walking out the door the dark-haired hiker said, "I'll be right back."

I walked to the front porch and saw that he was searching through an old looking canvas backpack.

"Here it is." He walked back to the porch and handed me the paper.

"If you go up there, be careful, it's purty rough."

"Thanks."

He turned to walk away.

"Hey, you guys don't need the map?"

"No. You can have it." He opened the rusty door to the pickup and started to get inside. His buddy started the engine and the lack of a complete muffler made it real loud.

I yelled out, "Does this trail go past an old abandoned cabin?"

He put his hands up to his ears telling me he couldn't hear as the truck pulled out of the lot. I went back inside and spread the paper out on the counter. It was a hand-drawn map and not in very good condition. It had landmarks drawn on it like a stream, a big rock, a cliff, a large oak tree, even a rock that looks like a butt, and a cabin.

Papaw walked in the front door and I quickly put the map into my pocket. I wasn't sure why I hid it, but I did. I went out back to play with Coty and I took him for a short walk. I studied the map while Coty bounced all over the place smelling spots, marking spots, and chasing bumblebees. I tried to warn him that he probably wouldn't enjoy catching one of them.

I heard Papaw call out from the porch that dinner was ready.

Coty and I ran back to the house. For dinner we had a pork roast, mashed potatoes, green beans and corn bread. Mamaw said she didn't have time to fix a dessert, but that she would have something made for this evening. She also said I could get a cake or something from the store if I wanted. I fed Coty and Leo the leftovers and I put the map in my nightstand and said goodbye. I grabbed a banana flip, let Coty loose, and we headed up the road to Susie's house. He walked beside me with his nose in the air looking up at me. I had to share my cake with him. When we got to the top of the hill I decided to cut across the woods and go by Miss Rebecca Simmons's house and let Bobby Lee play with Coty for a few minutes on my way to Susie's.

As we walked through the woods, Coty was having the time of his life. He was bouncing over fallen logs and running all over the place. I had to laugh just watching how much fun he was having. He looked like a fur ball bouncing on the forest floor. He looked up to find me and then turned right and ran head first into a large log. He fell unto his side and laid there. I started to run to him but then noticed him lifting his head and shaking it. Soon he was up and running again even though he staggered a little at first. I laughed and laughed at him. "You're going to have to watch those logs. They'll jump out right in front of you."

We exited the woods into a field that butted up to Miss Rebecca's yard. The field was planted with hay and we walked between the rows to the house. Bobby Lee came walking out of the side of the house and onto the porch. I yelled his name and he looked up and began waving both arms at us. I heard him call into the house and tell Miss Rebecca that we were coming. When we finally got to the yard, Bobby Lee met us, and Coty ran and jumped up on him knocking him to the ground. Coty licked his face and arms. "It looks like Bobby Lee is getting his bath," Miss Rebecca said from the porch. "It sure is nice that you came to visit and brought Coty for Bobby Lee to play with."

"I'm on my way to go swimming with Susie and thought I would stop by."

"That's very nice of you. He's a very good looking dog."

I shook my head in agreement. The large porch was on the western side of the house and faced out toward nine large oak trees that provided shade and breeze for the porch and house. When I say large, I mean very large. They looked a hundred feet tall to me. We sat in the porch swing and watched Bobby Lee roll around on the ground with Coty.

Miss Rebecca got up and said, "I'll be right back."

She soon appeared with a plate filled with cookies and some cherry Kool Aid for me and Bobby Lee.

"Thank you."

"Do you like cherry Kool Aid?"

"My favorite." The cookies were sugar with vanilla icing and sprinkles on top. They melted in my mouth.

Miss Rebecca went back into the house and brought out a bowl of water for Coty and had a few dog treats. I showed them how he had been taught to *sit* and also to *stay*.

"How do you like living here?" I asked.

"I like it very much. It does get lonely sometimes though. You're the first visitor we've had."

"Maybe, since you went to church today you'll meet more people and have more visitors."

"Perhaps we will."

We talked for a few more minutes and then I got up to leave. I thanked her for the treats for myself and Coty and told them that we would be back soon.

Bobby Lee wanted to know how soon.

I laughed and said, "Maybe one evening this week."

Coty and I walked up the long drive to the main road and we started down the long drive to Susie's house. When we got to the crest of the hill I saw Susie walking toward us. Susie and I waved at each other and Coty ran down the hill toward Susie. He ended up rolling most of the way as his head got too far ahead of his paws.

"Miss Simmons called to tell me you were on your way. I thought I would meet you and we could go on to the pond."

"Sounds okay to me. I thought the twins might be going with us."

"I asked them if they wanted to. They said that they were still mad at you for introducing them to Bobby Lee and that they didn't want to risk catching cooties from swimming in the same pond as you."

We had a great time swimming and talking and watching the birds around the pond. Susie had brought a small blanket and we sat and watched the big white clouds go by. We found different clouds that were shaped like things. Susie saw one that she thought looked like Mickey Mouse. I saw one that looked like a white dove. She spotted a butterfly cloud and I lied about how one looked just like an elephant. She looked and looked at it and never could see the resemblance. I then told her I had made it up and laughed at her. She ended up laughing and punching me in the arm.

Coty had found a comfortable spot in the grass to sleep. The long walk had tired him out. I told Susie about the trail that the two guys had told me about. We talked about the young pastor and that we liked him. We wondered if he would be voted in. I told her what Papaw had said about if he was breathing he would be voted in.

We spent nearly four hours together and it was so much fun. I didn't want it to end, but Susie said that it was getting late and that she thought I should head home. I walked her back to her house. I heard the twins inside warning everyone to be careful of the killer coyote in the yard. Clayton was back from the meeting and said that Pastor White was going to be our pastor. Susie and I clapped. Clayton said he would give me a ride home. I was glad, because I probably would have had to carry Coty most of the way. On the way, Clayton told me that he also liked the new young pastor.

It had been a good day.

12 THE THIRD KISS

The water felt good up to my waist. I was wading in Devil's Creek fishing for rock bass. I didn't think Devil's Creek was as good for fishing as North Licking Creek, but for some reason it was loaded with rock bass and sunfish. James Ernest had come over early this morning and wanted to go wading and fishing to beat the heat. It had gotten really bad this week. It was in the mid-nineties every day. We had played Wiffleball a couple of times, but only in the mornings, and we still ended up covered in sweat.

We decided to wade up the creek from the bridge and just keep going until we got tired. We didn't keep any of the fish. We were having a contest to see who could catch the most fish. Coty came with us and played around the shore chasing everything he saw move. He would get hot and jump in the water. He would get out and shake and off he would go chasing again. Coty was really growing and seemed very happy. Even Leo seemed to like him a little. I saw them sleeping together one afternoon.

Pastor White is moving in with Uncle Morton. He had an extra bedroom in his house and offered to let the Pastor stay with him. Uncle Morton said he would like to have some company around the house, and the pastor was going to pay him some rent. We would now be going to church every Sunday, and I didn't really mind at all. I knew that I would like Pastor White as long as he didn't have me quote verses in front of the church.

"I've got another one," James Ernest said proudly. He now led twenty-six to nineteen. I was going to have to get serious and catch up.

I caught two quick rock bass and then asked James Ernest, "What's up with you and Sadie." I could see him blush after I asked him.

"Not much. We take walks almost every other evening. She holds my hand."

"So I guess you like her pretty good."

"Yeah, I guess so," he continued, though looking a little sad. "She doesn't have a lot to choose from."

"Well, neither do you." I didn't know if that helped any.

He smiled at me and said, "You're right. At least she's cute."

"She is cute."

I caught another sunfish.

"Hey, you're catching up twenty-six to twenty-two," James Ernest said. We both continued up stream catching more small fish. We had the smallest hooks you could get a piece of worm on. Some of the fish we caught weren't much bigger than my little finger. We were having a blast.

"I've got to tell you something," James Ernest said a bit later, turning toward me.

He seemed so serious. I wondered what was wrong, was it his mom. He always had trouble with his parents. We had somewhat of another bond in that regard.

"Sadie kissed me on the lips."

"She did?" I wasn't at all surprised.

"That was my first time. It was weird."

He hesitated, so I jumped in, "What do you mean, it was weird?" I couldn't think of how a kiss could be weird.

"Have you kissed Susie on the lips?"

"I'll never kiss and tell."

James Ernest splashed me in the face.

"Come on, Tim!" James Ernest was almost begging.

"No. She kissed me last year on the cheek when I gave her the heart necklace. But we've never kissed on the lips. I don't know what would be weird about it if she did. I think I would like it."

"It just wasn't what I expected. The first kiss was soft and...."

"The first kiss!" I quickly interrupted. "You didn't tell me that there were multiple kisses."

"Three."

"Three!" I yelled. Coty looked at me like something was wrong.

"I guess she was on a roll. The first was nice and the second was a little longer." He was turning red before my eyes. I thought maybe the morning heat was getting to him. Then he said, "Then during the third kiss... she stuck her tongue in my mouth."

"What?" I had never heard of anything like that. "What do you mean?"

"I didn't know what to do. It was strange enough to have a girl kiss me. It was nice, but then to have her put her tongue inside my mouth was spooky."

"I don't get it. Did she just stick her tongue out like a frog and stick it in your mouth? Did you have gum in there that she wanted?"

"No, nothing like that. When our lips were together she just slid her tongue between her lips and then mine."

"No wonder you said it was weird." I stood there trying to imagine it happening. I couldn't.

"I asked her what it was she had done."

"What did she say?"

"She said it was called something. I can't remember. She said there was a name for it."

"Was it *frog kissing* or a *lizard kiss?*"

"It was some kind of foreign name like Irish or Spanish or something. I can't remember. I was too stunned. I just stood there in a daze. I felt kind of used."

I laughed at him without meaning, too. He looked at me and I thought he was mad at me for laughing, but then he laughed.

"Yeah, girls are strange. But I like something about them," I said.

"Yeah, me too."

We went back to fishing. Soon I was ahead in the number of fish caught and James Ernest never caught up. We quit around noon and began wading back toward the store. A gray crane was flying ahead of us. As we neared, he flew a little farther. We would catch up and he would fly some more. Coty was trying to catch a mink. The mink would just dive under the water. He seemed to be teasing Coty. Coty howled at him when he finally got frustrated.

We got back to the store and James Ernest went home. I

went inside and grabbed an RC Cola, and Mamaw said she would fix lunch for us. Papaw said he was going to West Liberty and asked me to stay inside and watch the store. He said he would wait until I got changed and we ate lunch.

We had lunchmeat sandwiches. I had pepper loaf with tomatoes and cucumbers on my sandwich. Papaw had ham and cheese and Mamaw decided to have a spam sandwich.

Papaw was backing the pickup out of the lot and Mamaw ran out.

"Buy me a new turkey baster. I'm not using the old one ever again."

"Okay," Papaw said, laughing and nodding.

The phone rang and Mamaw answered it and yelled, "It's for you Timmy. It's Randy."

"Hey what's up?"

"A Wolf Pack meeting tonight, at midnight, at the cabin. See you there." He hung up. It was exciting to think that we were meeting again. We always had small meetings, but had not had a secret meeting since the first one. It would be harder to sneak out of the window and get Coty without waking someone up. I didn't know if I should call James Ernest or if Randy would.

Mamaw walked out onto the back porch and I quickly dialed the phone number to James Ernest. He answered the phone.

"Did Randy call you?"

"Yeah."

"Let's camp out tonight in the backyard so we can sneak away easier."

"In this heat?" he questioned.

"It will cool down toward dark."

"Yeah, sure it will." I could hear the sarcasm in his voice. "I don't have to sneak out, remember."

"Yeah, but I do."

"Okay. I'll be there around dark when it's *so* much cooler."

I hung up the phone just as Mamaw walked back into the kitchen. "What's this about camping out tonight?" she asked me.

"James Ernest wants to camp out in the backyard tonight."

"In this heat?" she questioned.

"James Ernest says it will cool down toward dark."

"Yeah, sure it will. You boys are something."

I didn't want Mamaw to think I was out of my mind. I knew it would be hot all night. They were right. I didn't want to risk climbing out of the window with Coty. I was afraid we would wake them up.

I went back into the store and the mailman, Roger Smuckatilly, walked into the front door. I don't mean he opened it and walked in. He walked directly into the screen door. I heard him mutter something as I ran to the door and opened it for him.

"How long has that been there?" he asked.

"Only a few years," I answered.

"I thought so. I-I-I didn't ever remember it before." He was half lit on moonshine as always. I could smell the alcohol oozing from him.

"Do you go to that church with the new pastor?" he asked.

"Yes. You mean Oak Hills Church?"

Without answering he went on, "Is it true a man doesn't have to wear a tie or suit?"

"Yes sir."

"Well then, I might just attend. I-I-I don't have a tie or suit."

"I'll see you Sunday."

He left the mail on the counter and left through the same screen door he had left by for years and years. I looked down at the mail and noticed that we had a letter to the Tuttle's and also one addressed to Uncle Morton. I ran out the door with them in my hand just as Mr. Smuckatilly drove away.

That evening I put the tent up, much to Papaw's puzzled questioning. Around ten James Ernest arrived and we just sat in the lawn chairs and talked until it was time to head for the cabin. It was too hot to get inside the tent.

"By the way, I told my mamaw and papaw that sleeping out was your idea."

"Thanks a lot. You didn't want them to think you were stupid did you?"

"Yeah, something like that."

"Something just like that."

"Yeah," I finally agreed. He laughed and slapped me on the back.

We headed down the road to the crossover that went to the trail that led to the cabin. Coty was hot on our heels. I had my flashlight and my knife in my pocket. James Ernest brought nothing. I knew the guy was part dog. He could see in the dark just like a coyote.

We arrived at the cabin right at midnight and Randy and Purty were already there. Randy had brought a lantern instead of building a fire. I was thinking the whole way to the cabin about how hot it was going to be around the campfire. Sweat was already pouring off of me. I was glad we had smarter guys in the Wolf Pack than me. I even felt like Coty was smarter.

"Hey guys," Randy greeted us. "I see our new member also made it."

Purty was sitting near the lantern pit with nothing on except his shorts and a pair of tennis shoes. "Hey, nude man," James Ernest said to Purty.

"Randy made me wear the shorts. It's too hot for clothes," he explained.

"Let's all take off our shirts," I suggested, "unless the bugs get too bad." So we all took off our shirts and sat around the lantern. The bugs seemed to be drawn to the light of the lantern, so they left us alone. Coty laid between my legs. The walk tuckered him out and he wanted a night's sleep. He probably wondered what in the world we were doing hiking in the woods at night. I was wondering the same thing so I asked, "Okay, tell us what we're meeting about."

Randy looked at each one of us, in his way. He would stare into each person's eyes and then slowly turn his head to the next person. I wasn't sure why he did it, but it seemed to be something he liked to do, and it did set the mood to excitement. I never said anything about it. I just went along like the other guys.

After he completed staring in each of our eyes Purty said, "Aren't you going to look in Coty's eyes?"

James Ernest laughed and Randy said, "Coty is asleep, stupid."

Purty looked down at Coty and suggested, "He's awfully purty all curled all in the light from the lantern." Everyone looked down at Coty asleep between my feet.

"I was thinking that we need to have an adventure this summer. The Wolf Pack needs to do something out of the ordinary," Randy stated. "That is why I called this meeting. Playing Wiffleball every day isn't why we started a club."

Purty asked, "What do you have in mind?"

James Ernest and I both excitedly said, "Yeah, what?"

It sounded interesting to me. I was always up for something exciting. This summer had been fun, but not nearly as exciting as last summer. Of course I didn't want to find a dead body again, either.

"I don't know. That's why I called the meeting, to see if we could come up with something. All I could think of was to see if a parent could take us somewhere."

"Where could we go?" I asked.

Purty eagerly suggested, "Let's go to Hawaii. I've always wanted to go to Hawaii.

"Do you have a lot of money we don't know about?" I asked.

"I've always wanted to go to the Smoky Mountains. I hear it's real beautiful and all kinds of wildlife and big Black Bears everywhere," James Ernest suggested.

"Yeah, that's more like it. That would be fun," Randy agreed.

"It would still cost money though. I don't have much money and I know my parents couldn't send me any," I explained.

James Ernest agreed, "I don't have any money either."

"We could work for some money and save up and then go somewhere in August before school," Purty proposed.

"Where would we work?" Randy asked.

"We could work at the quarry, or for some of the farmers," said Purty.

Randy quickly rebuked him, "We have enough work around our farm that keeps us busy half the day."

Purty answered hurt and saddened, "Then we're just slaves in our own little world."

I looked at James Ernest and he looked at me and we both cracked up laughing at Purty. We both laughed harder and harder. James Ernest, while laughing, said, "We're just slaves—" But he couldn't finish because he was rolling on the ground laughing so hard.

Coty woke up and began barking and howling at James Ernest. I laughed until my sides hurt. Randy had tears from laughter and finally Purty even had to laugh at himself.

When James Ernest managed to stop laughing and rose from the ground he had dirt all over his back. I got up to help him clean it off. I reached into my pocket to get out a handkerchief to wipe the dirt and found a piece of paper. I remembered what it was, the map. I had put in my pocket to show the guys, but had forgotten about it with the talk of a great adventure.

I unfolded it and Purty asked, "What's that?"

"A map."

"A map of what," Randy asked.

"Trails." I told them about the two guys that came into the store and about how the one guy gave me the map. I told them how it started right where we were and ended up back here again.

Randy picked up the lantern and said, "Spread the map on the rock and let's look at it." I carefully laid it out and smoothed the wrinkles the best I could. Coty sniffed the map and then found a new spot to curl up.

"It looks like there are two different trails," Randy explained.

"Yeah, that's what the guy told me. He said the shortest trail takes two days to hike and the longest one takes four days. They said it was fairly rough hiking."

"Both trails are rough?" Purty asked.

"I don't know. They were on the four day trail. He didn't really explain. It all happened quickly and then they left. I couldn't believe he gave me the map," I said.

"This could be our adventure. We could take an overnight hiking trip," James Ernest suggested.

"I've never been on an overnight hiking trip," Purty said jubilantly.

"Me either," I said.

James Ernest echoed, "Me also."

Purty studied the map and soon laughed and yelled, "There's a rock that looks like a butt." Randy and James Ernest jumped back up to look. "I bet it's purty." Everyone laughed again at Purty saying a rock that looked like a butt was probably purty. It seemed so funny. Everyone was soon seated and Randy quieted everyone down.

"Let's do it," he said.

I asked, "Do what?"

"Let's take the hike. Since we don't have any money and no way of getting any without robbing the bank, let's take the hike. That would be an adventure." Randy then stood and announced, "The Wolf Pack will conquer the Big Butt Trail."

We all stood at once and began chanting, "Big Butt, Big Butt, Big Butt Trail! Big Butt, Big Butt, Big Butt Trail!"

We all sat back down on the rocks and I said. "What if my grandparents won't let me go overnight?"

"You could sneak out, like tonight," Purty suggested.

I looked at him and shook my head and explained, "They might just notice if I'm gone for two whole days."

"Oh, yeah."

"I'm the youngest, plus I don't want to lie to them."

"Will your parents let you two go?" James Ernest asked Randy and Purty.

Purty looked at Randy and Randy answered, "I think so, especially if everyone can go. There's safety in numbers. Can you?" Randy looked at James Ernest. James Ernest shook his head yes. I knew he could. His mom never seemed to care where James Ernest went to or where he was.

"Maybe you guys should get your parents and grandparents together and ask them at the same time. Show them the map and give them a plan, real professional-like, to show that we didn't just think it up," James Ernest said.

"Yeah, we'll trick them into saying yes," Purty said through his smile.

I had to admit that James Ernest's plan might just work. "You need to be there also, remember safety in numbers," I suggested to James Ernest.

"Okay."

We decided to confront them on the Fourth of July while everyone was in a good mood. We voted on the plan and it passed. Randy asked if anyone had any other business to bring up. He closed the meeting and we stood for our club chant.

We stood in a circle with Coty on the inside and howled to the sky like wolves again. We then jumped up and down five times chanting, "Wolf Pack, Wolf Pack, Wolf Pack, Wolf Pack, Wolf Pack"—one for each member. We bent down and held out our hands in the middle like a basketball team, I told Coty to shake, and he put his paw on top and we yelled, "Forever the Pack."

We all walked together to the turn off. Then James Ernest, Coty and I continued straight ahead listening to the night sounds. A hoot owl was shouting overhead and the tree frogs were noisy in the woods. The coolness of the night heat felt so much better without the sun's rays. When we got back we decided not to sleep in the tent. James Ernest went home and Coty and I climbed through the window to my bed and his cardboard den.

I prayed that Mamaw and Papaw would say yes to the hike and then I realized that Mom and Dad were coming for the fourth. It might be harder to convince them. I had forgotten they were going to be here. Soon my worry turned to sleep as the loud night sounds carried on outside my window without me.

13 FORGIVENESS

SUNDAY, JULY 3

I woke the next morning and looked forward to going to church. I wanted to hear Pastor White preach. I wanted to see Susie again. I had stayed around the store and helped the past two days. The heat was still just as bad. On Friday, Mamaw did the wash and hung the laundry out on the line in the backyard like she always does. There was a good breeze blowing, and the laundry was whipping in the air.

Coty took this as a sign that the laundry wanted to play. Apparently he grabbed every bit of clothing that he was able to jump up to and pulled them off the line. Once they weren't whipping around he became disinterested and left them on the ground. Mamaw walked out of the kitchen to the back porch and caught him trying to fetch the end of her brassiere.

"Stop that! Stop that!" She grabbed the broom off the porch and took off after him. He whimpered and ran out of the yard toward the front porch. I was in the store when Coty came to the front screen door crying and shaking. I asked him, "What's wrong little guy?" Papaw seemed concerned until Mamaw came into the store with an upset look on her face.

"You guys are just going to have to wear dirty shirts and pants. I am not going to wash them again. Next time I'll get the rifle and shoot me a coyote." Mamaw ranted on and on, and then she explained what Coty had done. Papaw and I waited until she was back on the back porch before we started laughing. We knew Mamaw loved Coty like we did.

"You had better go help pick up the clothes," Papaw told me.

So I spent Friday keeping Coty away from Mamaw. Later that evening during supper Papaw got Mamaw to laugh about it. She said it was actually kind of cute seeing him jumping up trying to catch her brassiere in the wind.

Early Saturday morning Mom called to say that they would not be coming for the holiday. She said Dad was still not feeling well. She told me she was sorry and would call me again soon to let me know how Dad was doing. Last year all my aunts and uncles came for the Fourth of July. This year no one was coming. Robert and Janice invited all their neighbors to come to their house to celebrate the fourth. I wasn't sure who all would be coming.

Robert and Janice came to pick Mamaw and me up for church. James Ernest jumped into the car and rode with us. When we arrived at church I noticed right away that none of the men had on suits or ties. The building was almost full. There were even more people there than last year when I said my memory verses. It was hot outside, but the pastor had gotten more fans placed inside the church to keep it as cool as possible.

Pastor White began the service with prayer. "Good morning Father. I thank you for this church, this body of believers gathered in Jesus our Lord's name. I pray for the word of God to be proclaimed today and for you to add increase to the body of believers. Thank you for your faithfulness and grace. May you see our joy as we worship, in the name of your son Jesus Christ I pray, Amen."

He then began singing and motioned for everyone to stand and join. I didn't want everyone to join. I wanted to listen to Pastor White sing. After we sung he had all the kids nine and under to come forward and sit around him. The twins, Thelma and Delma, were the first up on the stage and then Bobby Lee plopped down right next to them. Others soon followed. He told them about David and Goliath. He told them how all the other soldiers were scared and were without the faith they needed. But David believed his God would be with him and he killed the giant and held his head up for all to see.

At that moment the twins yelled out, "Gross."

Pastor White laughed and then said, "Sometimes the Bible isn't pretty, but neither is our sin." He had the kids return to their seats and continued preaching on sin and the effects of sin on a person's life. He told how a sinner can have all their sin removed by accepting Christ as their Lord and Savior. He quoted John 3:16 and some verses from Romans and gave an invitation for anyone to come forward and talk to him about accepting Christ.

The church was so quiet. All I could hear was the sound of the fan's blades cutting the air. "Now is the time to accept God's mercy and love," Pastor White stated. I heard footsteps coming up the center aisle of the small church from near the back of the church. I turned my head and looked; most others had their heads bowed. Slowly walking forward with tears streaming down his cheeks was Roger Smuckatilly, our mailman. As he neared the front of the church to where Pastor White stood with open arms a lady followed behind with even more tears covering her face. It looked like someone had busted a water balloon on her face.

Pastor White knelt with Roger and a large woman left her pew to kneel with the lady. After a few minutes Pastor White announced that Roger and his wife Lily had both just accepted Jesus Christ in place of their sin. The church erupted in clapping and shouts of *amen* and *hallelujah*.

Before the Pastor closed in prayer he announced that he was going to begin an evening gathering for all school kids, ninth grade and below, on Wednesday evenings. He said there would be games and snacks and lots of fun. He said it would begin at seven that Wednesday. He also needed some volunteers to help, especially a couple of kids in high school.

Then he prayed, "Father, thank you for adding to the body of Christ these two saints. I know it's not because of their goodness but only because of your goodness and sacrifice that today we can call them our brother and sister. Thank you, Amen."

Most of the adults hurried forward to greet Roger and Lily. James Ernest and I found our way through the crowd and out the front door. Susie and Brenda were close behind us.

"Do you think you'll come Wednesday night?" I asked Susie.

"Yes, it sounds like fun. We've never had anything just for kids," Susie answered.

"Are you going to come, Brenda?" James Ernest asked.

"Maybe," Brenda answered. Brenda was twelve and would soon turn thirteen. She was one year ahead of James Ernest in school and would be entering the ninth grade that fall. Susie and I would be entering the sixth grade and James Ernest would be in the eighth grade.

Daniel Sugarman ran up and said, "Hi, you guys going to come Wednesday evening?"

"Yes," everyone answered.

"See you then. I have to go. Bye." Daniel "Spoon" Sugarman went off running.

"Is everyone going to Robert and Janice's tomorrow for the party," Susie asked.

"Yes," everyone answered again.

"Let's all go swimming this afternoon," I suggested.

"Where?" James Ernest asked.

Susie suggested, "Let's go to the Collins' swimming hole. We can take a picnic for lunch and go right away. Get cooled off from this heat."

"I like this idea," James Ernest said.

"Me, too," I said.

Susie turned to Brenda and pleaded, "Come with us, Brenda. Have some fun."

She thought for a bit and then said, "Let's ask Mom."

Monie agreed and said she would put together some food that she had already prepared for dinner. Mamaw said she would throw together some lunchmeat and a loaf of bread and some snacks. James Ernest wanted to know if he could call Sadie and ask her to come. Monie said that she and Mamaw were going to can pickled beets at the store this afternoon so she was glad the girls were doing something.

"Sure," I said, "and see if the Randy and Todd can come. We'll have a party."

Within an hour all the kids were inside Mamaw's kitchen putting all the food into a basket and we grabbed soda pops to drink. Randy, Todd, and Sadie brought their eight-year-old sister, Francis, with them. Brenda and Susie were there. The twins said it was too hot to be outside and stayed at the store playing with their Barbie dolls. James Ernest brought a whole chicken that his mom had made for their dinner. We had a feast and we looked like a parade walking around the lake with Coty leading the way. Only a couple of fishermen were there due to the heat. They stared at us as we marched around the west side of the lake.

Everyone quickly stripped down to their swimming suits and jumped into the pool. It was crowded with so many in the pool, but it was so much fun. After Coty had jumped in and cooled off, he found some shade and quickly went to sleep. Sadie brought a small beach ball and we played keep-away, boys versus the girls. The girls had a hard time getting it away from us unless Brenda got hold of the guy with the ball. Sadie wore her two piece swimming suit and I heard Susie tell her, "I would like to get one, but I'm sure Mom wouldn't let me."

The pool seemed less crowded and I looked around to see Randy and Brenda sitting on a towel talking to each other. They seemed to have hit it off. I looked at Randy sitting there. He had a rugged, handsome look to him. He was tall and had black wavy hair. I was sure girls thought he was good-looking. He was always sure about himself. He tried he act older and wiser than everyone else. I had learned during the summer that he also had a kindness to him that he tried to hide.

Francis had taken a liking to me and she kept hanging on my back with her arms around my neck choking me. The only way I could get her off was to duck her under the water until she let go. I did it and made my way over to Susie.

"It looks like Randy and Brenda are getting along."

"Yeah, I'm surprised. I didn't think she would ever tolerate a guy."

"Why?" I asked.

"She never has anything good to say about boys," Susie explained. We were watching them talk and all of a sudden Randy bent over toward her as if he was going to kiss her. She jerked her head away and I could see her right arm swing from her side and belt him hard in the stomach. She then slowly stood up and dove back into the pool. Randy just sat there dazed. Randy raised his head and stared at her and then he glanced toward Susie and me. He knew we had seen what happened by the look on our faces.

He grinned at us as he blushed, and then he dove into the pool following her. Sadie and James Ernest were splashing each other and Purty was leaning against the side of the pool looking up into the sky with a grin on his face. I didn't want to know what he was doing.

We decided to eat lunch. Susie and I got out and spread all the food out on a towel that we had placed on a flat rock. As we were eating Fran said, "Thanks for letting me come along. I'm really enjoying this." Francis was a little chubby like her brother, Todd. She had the same sandy-colored hair that he did. It seemed like the kids either took after their mom or dad. There was no in-between. Francis and Todd took after their father and Sadie and Randy after their mother.

When we were almost done eating Purty asked, "What if we play spin-the-bottle?"

"No," everyone yelled.

"Let's go skinny dipping then."

"No," everyone yelled.

Randy was sitting next to Brenda again. They were talking and laughing. I hadn't seen Brenda ever laugh so much. She seemed to enjoy being around Randy. We all jumped back into the pool and began a game of tag. We played tag until everyone got tired of it and then everyone lounged near the edge as the pool. Some were sitting with their feet in the pool and others were in the pool hanging on to the sides.

Purty and Fran were hanging out with Susie and me. Randy and Brenda were talking again and Sadie had all of James Ernest's attention.

"I'm really looking forward to our two-day hike," Purty spouted off.

"What hike?" Susie asked.

I rolled my eyes at Purty, but he continued as if he didn't see me. I knew he wanted to talk about it and nothing was going to stop him. "Our club is going to go on a hike for a club activity," Purty continued.

"Where are you guys going?" Sadie asked.

Quickly I tried to control the damage. "We're not for sure if we're going. We haven't asked yet."

Purty kept talking. "Timmy's got a map and it has a trail that takes two days to hike. It starts at the cabin and goes up to Blaze and back. There's a rock that looks like a butt. I can't wait to go. I bet it's purty."

"You bet what is pretty?" Susie asked.

"The rock that looks like a butt," he answered.

"I think you're a sicko. Why are you so obsessed with nudity?" Susie asked. Everyone laughed because we all knew it was true.

Purty laughed also and then tried to explain. James Ernest

and Sadie moved over next to us to hear Purty explain it. "I'm not sure. I know it feels good to me to be naked. It's such a freedom. I also think the body is really neat. Maybe I'll be a doctor or a coroner. Some countries people walk around naked all the time. I've seen them in National Geographic magazines. I've heard that people sunbathe naked on the French Riviera."

James Ernest poked me in the ribs under the water. I looked at him and he motioned me away from the others. Purty was continuing his praise of nudity like he was a preacher talking about God. I swam away with James Ernest and he said, "That's what it's called."

"What?" I asked him.

"French kiss. That's what Sadie called it."

"Called what?"

"When she stuck her tongue in my mouth, she called it a French kiss. Remember, I couldn't think what she called it," he explained.

"Oh yeah, you mean the frog kiss." I laughed and then I laughed harder. The whole thing struck me as so funny. Purty was holding court on the virtues of nudity and James Ernest was explaining that kissing like a frog was called a French kiss. Randy had gotten socked for trying to give Brenda a small kiss. I couldn't help but laugh. James Ernest splashed me and went back to Sadie's side.

When Purty finally quit talking Susie said, "I want to go also."

"Where?" Brenda asked.

"I want to go on the hike. I've never done anything like that. It sounds exciting and fun."

Sadie agreed, "I think so too. I want to go also. What about you Brenda?"

"Sounds like fun," Brenda said.

"That would be fun," Purty said.

Randy looked at Brenda and smiled and said, "I would like that."

James Ernest had went mute again as he looked at Sadie.

"No! No way!" I yelled. I surprised myself with how forceful I said it. I couldn't believe what I was hearing.

Susie turned and looked at me and asked, "Why not? What's wrong with us going?"

I knew I was in a mess. I knew someone was going to get mad. It would probably be Susie. So, of course, I went on like an idiot.

"It's a boy's club. No girls are allowed in our club and this is our club's adventure. It's for our members. We can't break our rules already."

"There's nothing in the rules that say we can't have guests on our adventures. They just can't be members," Purty argued.

Our other two members, Randy, our pack leader, and James Ernest, were awfully silent for some reason. "True, but this is our first adventure. Besides, the parents won't let the girls go on an overnight hiking trip. Get real."

"What's the difference between you guys and us?" Brenda said as she stared daggers in my eyes.

"A lot," I said. "It would have to be a unanimous vote and my vote is no! If they go, I won't."

Susie looked at me dumbfounded. I felt so sorry for having her in the middle of it. It really had nothing to do with her. I would love to go on a hiking trip with her. But this was different. This was a bond between guys, a pact between us, and a chance for us to do something together, just the four guys and Coty. A time to be spent just being ourselves. Not trying to impress girls. Not letting girls come between us. If Purty wanted to hike naked, he could. We could fart, pick our nose, or belch, and no one would care. We could whip it out and pee *anywhere* we wanted to. This was something that we four would remember for the rest of our lives, as the Wolf Pack, not the Wolf Pack plus the three girls that tagged along.

I looked around and everyone was looking at me like I was the biggest jerk in the world. I climbed out of the pool, put on my shoes and walked away. Coty, who at the time felt like my only friend, walked with me. I walked up the stream and climbed the hill to the top of the cliff. I laid on a mossy rock near the cave entrance under a tree. Coty flopped down beside me and placed his head on my arm.

I felt a little sad, but at the same time I felt strong and proud of myself for taking a stand for what I believed in. I wondered if I was wrong. I wondered if Randy or James Ernest felt the same way, but were too scared to say. I began thinking about the cave and last year. I had wanted to take the Wolf Pack down into the cave. It would be fun to show them the cave with the bats.

I heard someone walking up the hill. I sat up to see Susie walking up the trail. Coty left my side and went to greet her. She followed him back to where I was. I was sure she was mad at me and was going to tell me so.

She started, "I'm sorry. I shouldn't have suggested for the girls to go along. You were right. You guys have your club and you should go by yourselves. If we girls had a club and planned something, I'm sure we wouldn't want you guys butting in."

I started to say something, but she continued before I could. She surprised me with her apology. "After you left, I thought about what you had said and knew that I was wrong. So I told the others that you were right."

"Thank you. It had nothing to do with you. I would love to go hiking with you. Maybe after we get back, if we're allowed to go, we could go for an all-day hike. Maybe we could take the same trail, but only go part way and then come back."

"You would know which part of the trail was the prettiest, or as Todd would say, *the purtiest*."

"Okay. I'm so glad you aren't mad," I said.

We sat there for few seconds and then Susie asked, "What were you laughing at James Ernest about in the pool."

I told Susie about Sadie kissing James Ernest and how on the third kiss she stuck her tongue in his mouth.

"She did what?"

"That's what I said," I said.

I then explained that he couldn't remember what it was called and that he had just thought of it when Purty was talking about the French. "It's called a French kiss."

"I've heard of a French kiss. But I didn't know what it was. It sounds weird."

"Yeah," I agreed.

"It feels nice up here on top of the cliff. There's a breeze blowing away some of the heat."

"Yeah, but I'm ready to cool off in the pool again."

"Okay, me too."

We got up and walked back to the pool with Coty.

14 "Amen"

I got up and did my chores. I slowly walked around the lake picking up the garbage from the weekend's fishing. We were supposed to be at the Easterling's by four in the afternoon. I had the day to kill until then and decided to do some fishing. I hadn't done nearly the amount of fishing that I had last year because of the club. I grabbed some worms and my rod and reel. I went inside to tell Mamaw and Papaw what I was going to do.

Papaw said, "Keep some of the fish. We'll clean them and put them in the freezer for supper in a couple of days."

"Okay." I went to the slanted rock and sat down. I then cast my line into the deepest pool that I could reach with my night crawler. It was nice being alone. I wondered about my dad. I wondered what Mom and Janie were doing and how they were making out.

I wondered why Dad was always drinking. What made him go away and get drunk? I suspected he didn't like us for some reason. Perhaps he didn't like Mom, or maybe he didn't want kids bothering him. I knew he didn't like his job, even though he was very good at it. He painted houses and rooms for a living. He always came home with paint spots on his clothes.

When he didn't smell like alcohol he smelled like paint thinner or turpentine.

Why does a man want a family, and then not want to be with them or do things with them? Our family never did anything together except maybe go for an ice cream once in a while. We moved all the time. I went to two different schools in kindergarten, one in Michigan and one in Ohio. First grade was Kentucky. Second grade was Lincoln Elementary and Garfield Elementary schools. Third grade was Garfield and Washington Park Elementary in Virginia. Fourth grade was three different schools, some that I had already gone to. I had hit almost all the Presidents.

Finally in the fifth grade I got to stay in one school for an entire grade, even though we moved three times. All the houses were in the same neighborhood. But my mom was always there for us. I felt sorry for her. I wondered if she felt the same as I did. Did she wonder why Dad didn't want to be at home and enjoy his family?

I caught a two pound bass and a few large bluegills before I headed back to the house. Papaw helped me clean them.

"What makes a man want to get drunk all the time?" I asked Papaw.

Papaw glanced over at me and said, "I don't know. I think it just gets in his blood. I don't even think he wants to. It just beckons him and he goes. It's a sin that is hard to stop."

I thought about that for a minute and then asked, "Do you think Mr. Smuckatilly will stop drinking now that he went forward at church?"

"He might. It could be hard for him. But I think he'll try."

We finished cleaning the fish and placed them in the

freezer. I went into my bedroom and took my Bible from the nightstand drawer and opened it to the back part and read some of the words written in red. I felt as if the Bible was really hard to understand in most parts. It seemed as if God could have written the Bible in an easier way to understand. Of course if you looked at my grades, I had a hard time understanding any book.

Soon I was asleep for an afternoon nap.

Mamaw woke me up and said for me to get ready. It was almost time to go to Robert's for the Fourth of July party. I changed clothes and ran out to get the Wiffle balls and bats. I thought we might have a big game with bases and everything. Papaw said that Coty could go with us. Papaw was closing the store for the rest of the day. James Ernest went with us.

We arrived a little early, because Mamaw wanted to help Janice get ready for everyone. Janice said that almost everyone was coming. Homer and Ruby were already there and Uncle Morton came with Pastor White. I was glad to see the Pastor there. Forest and Loraine Tuttle came in their van and all six kids climbed out. This was going to be so much fun. A small car drove down the lane and I recognized it as Miss Rebecca Simmons's car. I ran to meet them and Bobby Lee hopped out and started playing with Coty.

"Hi, Miss Rebecca."

"Hi, Timmy. I am so glad to be here. This is going to be so much fun."

"It sure is."

Dana and Idell were there. Tammy was helping her mom in the kitchen. Finally I saw Clayton's red pickup coming down the lane. I ran up to it and helped Susie down. "You guys are late."

"The twins couldn't decide what to wear. I almost left them home," Monie said frustrated.

The twins wore matching blue shorts with red and white striped tops.

"You two are very patriotic. You look like flags," I teased.

"At least we don't look like a doofus, like you," Delma came back.

"He does look like a doofus," Thelma added,

"What's a doofus?" I asked knowing it was not a compliment.

"Look it up in the dictionary. Your picture will be next to it as an example of one," Delma quickly said.

"I saw his picture there when I looked it up," Thelma said.

The twins were walking away and I said, "Have fun girls. Bobby Lee is here."

I heard Delma ask Thelma, "Who invited him?"

"Must have been a mistake, or maybe he crashed the party."

Bobby Lee looked up from playing with Coty and saw the twins and ran toward them. The fun was beginning.

I noticed Randy's youngest brother standing by himself. I figured he must not know anyone. Billy was seven and the same age as the twins. I yelled for him and motioned for him to come. Susie and I walked him over to the twins and Bobby Lee. They were in the middle of insulting each other. I introduced them to each other and ran for cover.

Susie and I ran over to where all the older kids had met up. We decided to wait for the sun to go down a little before we played Wiffleball. It wasn't long before the food was spread out and ready to be eaten. Robert asked, "Pastor White, would you ask the blessing for the food?"

"I'd be glad to. But one thing, I would like for everyone to call me Walker, instead of Pastor White. All my friends call me Walker." He went on to pray and then everyone dug in. There was enough food to feed the whole county. The women had made fried chicken, baked chicken, potato salad, coleslaw, corn pudding, fried apples, a baked ham, some kind of salad, baked beans, cornbread and homemade rolls. We had one table that was nothing but desserts. I saw the sugar cookies that I knew Miss Rebecca must have made. There were two picnic tables under a tree in the yard and all the older kids headed for them with their food. Pastor White walked over and asked if he could join us.

James Ernest in his deep voice looked at him very seriously and said, "These are very private tables Walker, sorry."

The pastor started to leave and we all laughed and told him James Ernest was just kidding. The pastor laughed and said, "That was a good one. That's a great voice you have, James. What a preacher you would make some day."

That was the first time I had ever heard James Ernest called just James by anyone.

"He has that great voice and this year was the first time I had ever heard it," I said.

"What do you mean?" the pastor asked.

So while everyone ate, James Ernest told the story about not talking. The Tuttle kids had never heard the story either. Everyone asked him all kinds of questions. James Ernest was the calmest and most eloquent that I had ever seen him. I believe the pastor commenting on his voice really gave him great confidence.

Miss Rebecca had joined the table because Bobby Lee wanted to sit next to me while he ate. She told James Ernest, "That is so amazing, that you could go that long without talking when all along you could. I would talk the first time I jammed my finger."

"Me too," the pastor said as he smiled toward Miss Rebecca.

"Mom would cuss the first time something happened," Bobby Lee added.

Miss Rebecca's face turned beet red and she said, "Bobby Lee, I do not cuss, shame on you for saying such a thing."

Bobby Lee added, "I've heard you say 'darn it' before."

The pastor laughed, and then we all did. The pastor said, "Bobby Lee, 'darn it' isn't cussing, although it is close. I've said worse than that myself." Bobby Lee quickly asked, "Yesterday, Mom was talking to Grandma on the phone and she told Grandma, 'Dang, he's the best looking preacher I ever saw.' Is that cussing?"

Miss Rebecca jumped from the table and headed to the house mumbling to herself. Pastor White said before she could get out of earshot, "Tell me more, Bobby Lee." Everyone at the table laughed and laughed. Idell lost all the food that was in her mouth on the ground. Sadie had Pepsi coming out of her nose.

After the table calmed down Susie asked, "I'm really excited about Wednesday evening. What all are we going to do Pastor White?"

He explained about games and snacks and some teaching and just talking about things. He said he would love to have the

Tuttle kids come. Everyone at the table said they were planning to come, except for the Tuttle's. Randy said they would have to ask their parents.

As soon as we were done eating we started a Wiffleball game. All the kids played including Bobby Lee and Billy. The twins decided they would try it. We talked Pastor White into playing and he talked Papaw, Robert, Forest, Clayton, and Monie into playing. Monie talked Miss Rebecca into playing. Uncle Morton asked if he could play. I told him he could be first base and everyone booed me and laughed at the same time.

We used the Rose of Sharon bush as first base. We found two rocks for second and third bases. I took off my Reds cap and used it for home plate.

Delma and Thelma had to be on the same team and they played the same position, right field. When Thelma batted in the bottom of the first inning she quickly struck out and declared, "This is a stupid game. We have better things to do." And off they went. It actually wasn't a great loss.

It almost seemed like the men and women were having more fun than the kids. The game was close and our team had the last at bat. We were losing twelve to eleven with the bases loaded and two outs. James Ernest was on third base, Billy was on second, and Tammy was on first. Miss Rebecca was up to bat and Randy was pitching to her. Randy threw the first pitch and Miss Rebecca swung and hit a line drive toward left field. It looked like a sure hit and we would win the game.

Pastor White was playing shortstop and he leaped high and sideways toward third and caught it with one hand. One of the greatest catches I had ever seen. Everyone applauded except for our team. Miss Rebecca couldn't believe it and took off running toward him. The Pastor was lying on the ground after making the catch. He saw her coming, and he quickly got up and took off running.

Mamaw said to everyone near her in the lawn chairs, "There's a sight that we will probably see for a while until she catches him."

My great Aunt Ruby said, "I don't blame her. If I was a little younger, I'd be chasing him too."

All the women said, "Amen." Then they all laughed.

After the game everyone headed to the dessert tables. I grabbed a large plate and filled it with cherry dumplings, sugar cookies, and a piece of coconut pie. I wanted a piece of chocolate cake but figured I'd go back later for it.

The Wolf Pack decided it was a good time to gather Randy and Todd's parents and my grandparents together to discuss our hike. We asked them to come to the kitchen table for a meeting. We made James Ernest go with us. We told him to remember, safety in numbers. Since Randy was the Leader of the Pack, we had him propose our plan. I pulled the map out of my pocket and spread it out on the kitchen table.

"Oh no. What is this all about?" Mamaw said as soon as she saw the map.

"Now Corie, let's wait and let the boys talk," Papaw told her.

"Okay Randy, what's up?" Mr. Tuttle asked.

Randy began, "As you know, we formed a club, the four of us."

I interrupted and added, "Coty is also a member." Susie and Sadie came into the kitchen and stood to the side.

"We would like your approval to take an overnight hike, the four of us," Randy continued.

Loraine began, "Oh no, that can't happen. There is no way we can let you two go off on a hike overnight. Anything could happen to you. You could be bitten by a snake, or bugs, or a bear. You could fall down and break a leg, or an arm, or a neck, or a finger. I would worry myself to death if I knew you were out there and possibly in danger. How could you two possibly come up with an idea of such proportions to worry me? I…" Forest interrupted her or she might have talked until morning light.

"Loraine we'll let Randy finish. But, I have to admit, I'm not too fond of the plan so far. Go ahead."

Randy went on finally, "There's a trail that starts at the cabin and goes up near Blaze and then back again. We would only have to camp out one night and we wouldn't be that far from home. We would be extra careful and carry all the supplies that we would need."

"I know of this trail. I've had folks come into the store either on their way or coming off the trail," Papaw told everyone.

"What do they say about it, Martin?" Forest asked.

"Well, I know there is also a four-day trail."

I pointed it out on the map. "Here it is, Papaw."

"The folks say that the four-day trail is pretty rough hiking, but they say the two-day hike is pretty nice and a lot safer. Some experienced hikers can hike it in a day."

"We want to do something exciting this summer and we don't have the money to go on a trip or anything. This is the best idea we could come up with," I said.

"I do like that it's not that far from the farm, and you boys are getting at the age where we need to learn to trust you," Forest said as he looked at Papaw.

"James Ernest, what does your mom say about it?" Mamaw asked.

"She doesn't care if I go. She's okay with it." I knew that his mom knew nothing about it. She probably would never know anything about it if we went.

"I guess I'll be okay with it if you let us make sure you have everything you need. Actually, when I was your age I would have really enjoyed a trip like this," Mr. Tuttle said. Loraine just wrung her hands and wanted to say something about her husband's decision, but Forest put his hand up to stop her.

"Don't you think we should call Betty and ask her what she thinks about this? Timmy is the youngest," Mamaw asked.

"I think Betty has enough worries without troubling her about this. Besides, last year Tim captured a murderer, I think he can handle a hike in the woods. He camps out in the backyard all the time." Papaw winked at me.

"When do you want to do it?" Forest asked.

"We hadn't really thought about that. We didn't think you would let us do it," Purty answered.

We all looked at Purty and shook our heads.

"It will take a while to get everything we need, and it might be best to wait till the summer heat breaks a little," James Ernest explained.

Papaw said, "That sounds good. Let's play it by ear and start working on getting what all you need."

Sadie stepped forward and said, "I want to go also. Can I go, Daddy?"

Forest answered quickly and decisively, "Absolutely not!"

That was all that was said about the girls going.

We were so excited that we were giving each other high fives and we did our Wolf Pack howl. We were actually getting to go on a two-day hike. I still couldn't believe it. James Ernest took the map and said he would make four good copies, one for each of us.

When we went back outside Pastor White and Miss Rebecca were playing games with all the smaller kids. They saw us and decided to form other games that we all could play. We had a blast playing all kinds of interesting games until it got almost dark enough for fireworks. Ruby yelled out that the homemade ice cream was ready, and we all ran to get some.

I had mine with a piece of the chocolate cake. Susie had a cone. We went and sat down together in the grass under a tree.

"Today has been a lot of fun," I told her.

Susie agreed and said, "I'm happy that you guys get to go on your hike. Sometimes I wish I was a boy."

"I'm glad you're not a boy."

"Why is that?"

"You know. I wouldn't like you as much if you were a guy," I tried to explain.

"Are you saying you like me, Timmy?"

I swallowed hard on a bite of cake and answered, "Yes."

She looked down at the ground and asked, "As a friend or as a girlfriend?"

"A girlfriend," I answered and the first firework went off above our heads.

15 GOOD GONE BAD

Caw, caw, caw, the crows called from the top of the trees out-side my open bedroom window. I awoke to the cawing and then heard a rooster crow in the distance. It had to have come from the Tuttle's farm. I picked up an Archie comic book, rolled it up and swatted a fly on the nightstand. It fell to the wooden floor. Other flies, as if alarmed by the killing, began swarming around the room. This was one of the hazards of having an open window during the summer, with no screen in the window. I would complain about not having a screen, except for the fact that a screen would make it much harder to sneak out during the night for our club's secret meetings.

I laid back down on the mattress and looked over the side of the bed at Coty in his box bed. He stretched and yawned and looked up at me. It seemed too early for even him to rise for the day. I began thinking of the Fourth of July picnic and Susie and I telling each other that we were boyfriend and girlfriend. It seemed a little strange, because I already considered ourselves to be that without saying it to each other, but it seemed to be important to her. I wondered if Sadie had the same conversa-tion with James Ernest.

This evening would be the first kid's night at the church and I looked forward to it. I was going to call Randy and Purty to

179

see if they wanted to go with me and James Ernest. Papaw said he would take us and then pick us up afterwards. The morning air was cooler than the past mornings, and I was hoping the summer heat was taking a break for a while. It would still be an hour or more before the sun rose over the hill and the rays would shine into my window. I listened to the black crows cawing and heard the other song birds chirping out the beginning of the new day. I knew that I would have to get up soon and get my chores done, because the guys would show up to play Wiffleball around ten.

I heard footsteps in the kitchen and then the back door open and close. I knew someone was up and heading to the outhouse. I thought about Roger Smuckatilly delivering the mail yesterday. He had a gigantic smile on his face. He told Papaw that he had never felt better. It was the first time I hadn't smelled alcohol oozing from him. He still delivered Papaw the wrong mail, but at least he was happy while doing it.

I decided to get up and take Coty out so we both could pee. It was light enough outside to see and Coty took off chasing a chipmunk at the side of the house. The chipmunk dove into a hole in the yard and Coty stood there bewildered that it had disappeared. He pranced back to me with his head held high as if he had rid the yard of all the big bad rodents. Coty then spotted a rabbit munching on grass near the shed and took off after it. The rabbit hopped quickly away into the bushes leaving Coty to sniff the spot from which it disappeared.

I walked toward the back door and Coty headed to the doghouse where Leo was still bedded down. I watched him as he found a spot next to him. He dropped and put his paw on Leo's leg. Leo didn't move. Mamaw was in the kitchen heating water for coffee and asked, "What would you like for breakfast, Timmy?"

"Maybe some eggs and bacon, that sounds good. BLTs sound good and pancakes with lots of maple syrup would taste good. Toast with blackberry jelly, and a big bowl of cherry dumplings would be perfect and I love waffles with well done link sausage."

"You're really a big help."

"Hey, I gave you lots of choices. I pretty much like everything you fix."

"That's true. You don't turn away much food. Maybe I'll fix chicken livers and onions for breakfast." I knew she was grinning as she said it, even though I was walking away and into the store to see Papaw.

Papaw was turning the open sign over and unlocking the front door. Fishermen sometimes would be at the door waiting for Papaw to open so they could buy bait and pick their spot around the lake. Early morning was always the best time to fish in the hot summer months. That morning no one was waiting.

"Mamaw is fixing us chicken livers and onions for breakfast this morning," I told him.

"It sounds like we may be fishing this morning."

I laughed and Papaw added, "The catfish are the only critters I know that would eat chicken liver for breakfast." Fishermen were always using raw chicken livers for fishing bait. The smell would attract the fish, or that was the thought. "Where's Coty?"

"He's lying in the doghouse with Leo."

"I'm really surprised at how Leo has tolerated the little guy. I actually think he likes him."

"I think he does too."

"I'm going to town this morning. It's probably time for you to get a haircut."

"Okay, but I want Razor to cut it."

"He's the only one around. We also can start looking for supplies for your hiking trip while we're in town."

"Can I see if James Ernest wants to go with us?"

"Sure. I'll call Mr. Tuttle and see what all he thinks you boys need. I better catch him before he leaves for work." Papaw went to the phone and dialed the rotary phone and listened as it rang. I could hear Loraine say, "Hello, Tuttle's."

"Hi Loraine, this is Martin at the store." That's all Papaw said for the next five minutes. Loraine talked and talked. Papaw even laid the phone down for a while to rest his arm and ear. I could hear her babbling on and on, and I had to put my hand over my mouth so she wouldn't hear me laughing. She finally hesitated for a moment and Papaw quickly picked up the phone and asked, "Is Forest still there?" It took her ninety seconds and twenty-two sentences to say, "Yes he is, I'll get him for you, Martin."

Papaw talked to Forest about what all he thought we needed for the hike, and they compared it to what we already had. Papaw wrote a list. Forest said he would be happy to split the cost of everything with Papaw. "That would be fair; I don't think we could get James Ernest's mom to chip in. No, I don't mind either, he's a good kid. Maybe I'll ask him to do some chores to pay it off."

Mamaw walked in as Papaw hung up and announced, "The liver and onions are ready. Come and get it."

"Yum, yum, I can't wait," I joked.

Papaw and I followed Mamaw into the kitchen to find fried eggs and crispy bacon and toast waiting for us. She even had blackberry jam on the table and orange juice poured. I dug in and said, "This is the best liver and onions I have ever had."

"Me too. I like them a lot better with eggs and bacon on them," Papaw followed.

Mamaw laughed and said, "Next time you might get gizzards."

"As long as they have eggs and bacon or maybe maple syrup on them, it's okay with me," I said.

Mamaw was gone all day yesterday helping Monie and Ruby start the process of canning pickles. Canning sweet pickles took ten days to do and they were fantastic. They were the best pickles I had ever tasted. They had to wash them and slice them and leave them in salt water for seven days. The last step was adding sugar, vinegar and pickling spices for twenty-four hours and then canning them. The women enjoyed getting together and canning. I think they enjoyed the gossip and there was plenty after the picnic.

When I finished with breakfast I went around the pond to pick up the garbage. Coty followed me and snooped around. When we got back Mamaw put out some food for Coty and Leo. Coty and I then went to the spring for a bucket of fresh water. I then swept the front porch and steps off. I ran up the hill to see if James Ernest wanted to go to town with us. He came to the door eating a peanut butter sandwich.

"Is that your breakfast?"

"Yeah, I like it."

I decided not to press it. I didn't think his mom ever fixed him breakfast or much else either. She generally didn't get up until ten or so. He followed me back to the store, and we went in to find Papaw. He said he was almost ready so we went out to the porch and waited for him. I told James Ernest that we were going to pick out supplies for the hiking trip at the general store and that I was going to get a haircut. He seemed excited about going. I don't think he ever went anywhere.

We climbed into the pickup and Coty stood on the porch and watched us drive away. He seemed so disappointed.

After our haircuts we walked past the general store. Papaw went inside while James Ernest and I walked on to the bank to see Mr. Harney and Miss Rebecca. Miss Rebecca gave us suckers. "Aren't we a little old to be given suckers?" I asked.

Miss Rebecca answered, "We're never to old for a good sucker," and smiled at us. "Are you two going to be at the church tonight?"

"Yes ma'am," we both answered.

"Bobby Lee and I will see you there then. It will be a lot of fun." I didn't know that Miss Rebecca was helping with the kid's night, but I was glad.

We made our way to the general store and Mr. Cobb said, "Hello Timmy, and who is this with you?"

I introduced Mr. Cobb to James Ernest and then we joined Papaw to look at the supplies.

"Martin says you boys are going on a hiking trip. Sounds like great fun."

"Yes sir," I said.

"You just have to be careful while you're out there."

"Yes sir," James Ernest answered.

Papaw picked out a compass, and Mr. Cobb taught us how to use it. Papaw said we should have a four man tent and Mr.

Cobb said he had one that was fairly light-weight that might be perfect for the four of us. He suggested we practice putting it up in case we had to do it in the dark. Papaw found a small hatchet that he thought we could use for hammering in the tent pegs and chopping fire wood.

"It's not for throwing at each other," Papaw warned. "You've got a knife and a flashlight. Forest said they had a lantern that you could use. I don't think you'll need sleeping bags, too hot. You can pack a couple of old sheets to sleep under."

Mr. Cobb suggested a first-aid kit and some waterproof matches. Papaw placed them with the rest of the stuff.

Papaw said, "I think that might do it for a one-night trip. You can take food and you won't have to cook any. No need for camp pans or skillets."

"What about backpacks?" I asked.

"You're right. You've got to carry this stuff some how."

I began looking at the backpacks and James Ernest just stood there. "You have to pick one out, James," Papaw said.

"No thank you, Mr. Collins."

"I'll pay for it and you can work it off, do some chores for me."

"No thank you."

"It's okay, James Ernest," I urged him.

"Thank you, but I don't need one." He turned and walked out of the store. I picked out a backpack and went outside to look for James Ernest while Papaw paid for the gear.

"Let's go swimming in the creek when we get back this afternoon."

"Okay," James Ernest said.

We drove back, and that afternoon we went to the creek

and played and swam. Coty played along the bank chasing the movements. Soon Randy and Purty found us. We talked about the gear we bought and the fun we were going to have on the hike.

The afternoon went by fast. I didn't mention James Ernest's refusal to get a backpack to him and he didn't mention it. After supper, Papaw took me and James Ernest over to pick up Purty and Randy for the kid's night. We were surprised when all the kids jumped into the truck bed except for three-year-old Trudy. Sadie climbed up in the back with Randy and Purty and sat next to James Ernest. Francis and her seven-year-old brother, Billy, climbed into the cab with Papaw. Loraine came out of the front door and waved and headed for the truck. Papaw saw her coming and quickly backed up and headed down the lane before she could reach the pickup. I heard her yell, "You all, be good...." and then her voice faded away.

"This isn't going to be all memorizing verses, is it?" Purty asked

"I don't know. I don't think so. We'll find out," I answered.

Sadie had on her pretty sundress. The same one she had worn when I took her for the walk and she tried to kiss me. Randy and Todd wore nice pants and button up shirts. I wore jeans and a button up shirt and James Ernest had on a t-shirt and bib overalls. I think they were his nicest pair though. We arrived just in time and most everyone was already there. The pastor had placed chairs outside under the trees. I saw Susie and Delma and Thelma. I saw Daniel Sugarman. Kids were there that I didn't know but had seen at church. Izzie Sargent was there. She was my age and I had gone to school with her in the first grade at the one room school. She was sitting with Susie.

Izzie had long brown hair down to her waist and a pretty smile. She always smiled at me and said hi. Even in the first grade. I would always say hi back, but I had never stopped and talked to her. Altogether, I counted twenty-five kids. I think it was almost everyone in the area. Another pickup pulled up and five kids got out. Daniel said they were from Blaze.

Pastor White was standing talking to Miss Rebecca, Tammy Easterling, and Brenda. Bobby Lee was standing in front of Delma and Thelma making faces at them. They were doing their best trying to ignore him. Mrs. Hazel Roberts was keeping a close eye on everyone. She was an older lady from the church whom must have volunteered to help out, and she had a look on her face like she had made the biggest mistake of her life. I figured she was thinking up an excuse to leave.

I walked over to Susie and said hi. "Do you remember Izzie?"

"Sure, we went to the first grade together," I said, looking at Izzie. "I see you at church most Sundays."

"I see you too."

"Your hair sure is long."

"I've never had it cut."

"Never?"

"No."

Pastor White then asked for everyone to be seated. He said he was glad to see that so many kids had come. He said that from now on everyone should wear old clothes for playing games. He said shorts were even okay. He said he was going to divide us in two groups. He asked the fourth graders and older kids to go with him and for the younger kids to go with Miss Rebecca and Mrs. Roberts. Tammy and Brenda stayed with our group. We all sat in a circle and Pastor White had us stand and introduce ourselves and tell our age, what our favorite color and animal was, and why.

He had Susie go first, "I'm Susie Perry, I'm ten, and my favorite color is blue. I guess because I love the blue sky. My favorite animal is a horse because I have one, and I love him." Susie then sat back down.

"Next," Pastor White urged.

Izzie stood and then Daniel and then a kid named Hiram. He was one of the boys from Blaze. He was twelve and he said he liked black and loved black snakes. I decided to stay away from him, for now.

James Ernest stood and began talking, and some of the kids giggled because of his deep voice. He said he was twelve, liked the color green, like grass, and like giraffes. Pastor White said, "And he has a great voice."

I stood next and said, "I'm Tim and I'm ten. I also like blue. I like to look up at the sky. My favorite animal is a dog because I have one named Coty."

Sadie stood next and said, "I'm Sadie Tuttle and I'm also ten. I love green because it's the color of James Ernest's eyes." Everyone laughed and James Ernest turned red. "I like deer because they have beautiful long eyelashes like I do." The boys laughed and the other girls just stared at her.

It was Purty's turn and he jumped up and said, "Hi, I'm Todd Tuttle and I'm twelve. I like the color pinkish-tan because it's the color of a naked baby when it's born, or a new born mouse or a little pig right after it's born and all naked. I think it's a real purty color." Randy reached up and jerked him down before he could name all the naked animals.

"Hey, I didn't get to tell about my favorite animal."

Hiram was overheard saying, "That's one stupid kid." Randy was one of the people that overheard him. It didn't take long for Randy to get up, run over and dive on the kid and start pounding him with all that he had. Everyone stood to get a better view. A girl from Blaze jumped on Randy's back and began hitting him. Pastor White quickly began shouting and trying to separate everyone.

Sadie was yelling, "Hit him again Randy! Hit him again!"

Brenda grabbed Sadie and told her to shut up. Sadie up and kicked her in the shin. Brenda was boiling mad and threw Sadie to the ground and sat on her chest so that Sadie couldn't move or speak. Tammy was holding onto the girl from Blaze. Pastor White finally got Hiram and Randy apart, and Hiram had blood flowing from his nose. Randy had scratches on his arms where Hiram had dug his fingernails into him like a girl. Pastor White then asked Brenda to let Sadie up.

Peace was being restored when suddenly I heard commotion coming from the younger kids. Half of them were watching our group and the other half were watching Bobby Lee and Billy while they were pulling the hair of Delma and Thelma. The twins were screaming bloody murder and Miss Rebecca was trying to pull them apart. Mrs. Hazel Roberts was throwing her hands in the air and crying. Susie and I backed away from the group. Susie looked at me and asked, "Do you think this is the last kid's night?"

"I don't think so. It sure seems like its needed real bad."

16 "Isn't God Good"

Randy, Purty, Billy and Sadie were punished for two days. I hadn't seen them since kid's night. Papaw told me that Mr. Tuttle was furious when he heard about it. Mamaw said that Loraine had gone straight to the apple tree, broken off a switch and used it on the four on them. I was sure Randy had more scratches on him now.

Pastor White said that he would announce when the next kid's night would be. I figured it would be a while. He ended up having all the kids sit facing him and he taught a lesson from the Old Testament about a man whom God told to sacrifice his son. I think Pastor White came up with that lesson on the spur of the moment. That was punishment enough to a group of kids. We played word games after the lesson; he said he didn't think we should play the physical games he had planned. Overall, I had a pretty good time.

Susie called last night and asked if I wanted to go swimming this afternoon at the Collins' pool. She said she would have to bring the twins. I told her that was fine. Her parents and Brenda were going to town and she had to watch the twins.

They arrived around one and we headed for the pool. Coty walked between Susie and me. As we walked, the twins began talking about the fight.

"That Billy Tuttle is meaner than Bobby Lee," Thelma said.

"He's plumb evil, that kid is," Delma agreed.

"What caused them to pull your hair?" I asked.

"Miss Simmons had each of us stand and say our name, age, favorite color, and what we liked to do," Thelma answered.

Delma interrupted, "I got to go first. I told them my favorite color was purple and I liked to color."

Thelma continued, "I went next and said that I liked purple also and I liked to color and play with our Barbies. Francis went next and then a girl from Blaze named Henrietta. Bobby Lee stood and said he liked the color purple because we did and that his favorite thing to do was play with us."

Delma went on, "I corrected him and said that we never played together and told everyone that he just liked to pester us. He stuck his tongue out at us and flopped back down. Billy then stood and said he liked to throw rocks and that his favorite color was dishwater blonde, the same color as our stupid hair."

"I said that he and Bobby Lee were the rudest boys on earth," Thelma told us.

"I said *Amen* and told them they were stupid little bugs. Billy reached over and grabbed my hair."

"Bobby Lee jumped up and got behind me and started pulling my hair. Miss Simmons was trying to pull them off which meant they were pulling our hair even more."

"Why was Mrs. Roberts just standing there crying," I asked.

"We don't know. She was no help at all," Delma said.

"We know that we don't like people that just pester all the time," Thelma continued.

Susie and I laughed at them.

"What's so funny?" the twins asked.

We were near the pool by then and I ran and jumped in. Coty jumped in right beside me. Susie followed and we had a grand time splashing and swimming and playing games. The twins continually pestered me. Once they stuck behind me while I was talking to Susie and put a big rock down the back of my pants. I began sinking. I finally managed to pull it out.

"I could have drowned."

"That was the plan."

"Yes. Of course you did. That was our plan."

Delma looked at Thelma, and Thelma said, "We need to find a bigger rock."

"Good idea," Delma said with a sly smile.

I took off chasing them and dunking them, and everyone laughed and laughed.

After an hour or so of playing with the twins Susie and I got out and laid on the towels we brought and looked up at the blue sky. We didn't speak for a while and then Susie asked, "When is the big hiking trip?"

"We haven't got a date yet. Randy and Todd have been grounded since kid's night so we haven't been able to talk. Papaw took James Ernest and me to town to buy stuff that we needed."

"It should be a lot of fun."

"Yeah." The sky was a deep blue and looked even deeper when you looked up through the limbs and leaves of the trees. A gentle breeze rustled the leaves giving us a nice sound to listen to. Coty was lying between us and was continually being petted by both of us. Our hands would touch every once in a while when we petted the same spot, it reminder me of last year when she held by hand after I found Mrs. Robbins dead.

Susie asked, as if reading my mind, "Do you think about finding Mrs. Robbins very much?"

"Yeah. Every time I go up to the Tuttle's house I think about her. When I go to bed I usually think about her before I go to sleep. When I see a garden or a picket fence I think about her. When Mom or Mamaw use a skillet I think of her being killed."

"Do you think she's happier now that she's in heaven? Maybe she's with her husband in heaven."

"I guess so." I thought about heaven for a while and then said, "What if there isn't a heaven?"

"Why would you say that?" Susie asked.

"Maybe long ago people just made it up. You know, like the Easter Bunny or the Tooth Fairy. Maybe people just wanted to have another holiday so they made up Jesus and heaven."

"I wonder why they made up things for kids to believe in."

"I don't know unless they did it just because they're fun."

Susie said, "Wouldn't Christmas be just as much fun if we gave gifts to each other because the wise men gave gifts to Jesus to show their love. Why do we need Santa Claus sliding down a chimney?"

"I always enjoyed Santa Clause. I still do," I said as I smiled thinking about Santa.

"Me too. Even though I know he's not real. We still talk about Santa coming."

"Don't the twins still think Santa is real?"

"No. Not since they snuck out of their room when they were four and hid behind the sofa all night waiting for Santa to come. Early that morning they saw Dad placing gifts around the tree. They jumped out from behind the tree and yelled, 'You're not Santa.' It scared Dad so bad that he fell forward into the tree and then onto the presents. All of our packages were wrinkled and crumbled that year."

I laughed.

"It wasn't funny at the time. Dad said he tried to make up something to tell them. He came up with a story about how Santa had eaten too many cookies during the night and he couldn't fit down the chimney so he left the presents on the porch. He said Santa had left a note telling him to put the presents under the tree for him. The twins then asked to see the note. When Dad said he threw it away the twins asked him where he threw it. They were going to go through all the garbage cans to find it so Dad finally confessed. The twins were more upset that Mom and Dad had tricked them for three years than that Santa wasn't real. I don't think they cared as long as they got gifts."

We laid there and giggled at the thought of the whole episode. Finally I asked, "So, do you think they made up heaven just so we'll be good."

"No. I hope not. I like thinking we'll end up in heaven together someday."

"Me too."

We got up and jumped back into the pool and played with the twins until Brenda showed up and said it was time to go home.

I looked at Brenda and said, "My favorite part of Wednesday night was when you sat on Sadie." We all laughed.

"I enjoyed that part too." Brenda smiled.

We all walked back to the store and Clayton and Monie invited us to come to their farm for dessert that evening. They were going to call others and said they just wanted to enjoy the company of everyone on a nice summer night.

I was glad that I was going to spend more time with Susie. We ate supper and then around seven-thirty we headed to Clayton's farm. We were the last to arrive. Papaw never liked to close the store too early. Robert and Janice were there with Tammy. Homer and Ruby had brought Uncle Morton. Uncle Morton said the pastor was finishing up his sermon for the morning and decided not to come. Miss Rebecca had come with Bobby Lee. Coty came with us and ran to Bobby Lee when he saw him. Bobby Lee began rolling around in the yard with him.

The women were in the kitchen getting the desserts ready. The men were on the porch talking about the weather and drinking sweet ice tea. The full moon was already rising and would be high in the sky by dark. The breeze still blew across the fields of corn and tobacco that surrounded the farmhouse. Susie and I headed to the field where her horse, Mr. Perry, and the goats were. The baby goats from last year were grown and there were new baby goats running around.

We returned to the house just in time for the desserts to be served, but before they were served, Miss Rebecca said that Bobby Lee had something to say. Bobby Lee stopped playing with Coty and slowly walked over to Thelma and Delma. He then turned and looked at his mom. She threatened, "We'll go home right now."

At a snail's pace he turned back around to face the twins and said, "I'm very sorry that I pulled your hair."

Miss Rebecca urged him on, "And why are you sorry."

Bobby Lee thought about it and answered, "Because I'll have to go home without dessert if I'm not."

Everyone cracked up laughing, even Miss Rebecca, and Bobby Lee ran back to play with Coty. Miss Rebecca didn't press the issue.

Thelma looked at Delma and stated, "That certainly wasn't much of an apology."

"It certainly wasn't. I'm not sure if it actually was one."

"It reminds me of some apologies I've heard from you two," Monie said.

Mamaw had made her cherry dumplings. Monie had made blackberry cobbler and a chocolate cake. Ruby brought banana pudding covered with vanilla wafers and Janice made strawberry ice cream. Miss Rebecca brought the tallest butterscotch pie I had ever seen. I wanted everything. I decided to start with blackberry cobbler with some strawberry ice cream on top. Susie had a piece of the butterscotch pie and we went out in the yard and sit on a blanket. The sun was setting over the western hills and the full moon was taking over the job of providing light. We laid down on our backs and looked up at the moon and talked about what it would be like to fly to the moon.

"I wonder if we were lying on the moon and we looked at earth if it would look the same as looking at the moon."

"Maybe, but it would be different."

"How?"

"Little green men would be chasing us."

"Very funny," Susie said. Then she asked, "Do you think anyone will ever walk on the moon besides little green men?"

"No."

Before we knew it Bobby Lee, Thelma, Delma, and Coty

joined us on the blanket. Everyone was lying there looking up at the moon. Bobby Lee finally asked, "What are we looking at?"

"The man in the moon," Susie answered.

"I don't see any man in the moon."

Susie tried to show Bobby Lee the face in the moon, but he wasn't buying any of it. "I might be a little kid, but I ain't dumb."

The twins held there tongue and didn't say anything. "Some people say the moon is made of cheese," I told them.

He jumped up and ran to Miss Rebecca complaining, "They think I'm stupid, Mom."

The twins soon grew tired of looking at the moon and left also. Susie slowly moved her hand over to mine and we held hands and gazed at the big bright full moon in the great big night sky and all was wonderful. Not another word was spoken between us for the next half hour. I just laid there and smiled.

We finally got up and went back for more dessert. I had to have some cherry dumplings. We went to the porch where all the adults were sitting. Car lights came over the hill and down the lane toward the house. We were excited to see who was coming. Homer said it looked like the pastor's car. Pastor White got out and said, "I sure hope you have some dessert left, or did Timmy eat it all."

"He tried, but even he couldn't eat it all," Papaw said.

"Follow me, Pastor. I'll get you a plate," Monie told him.

When the Pastor came out to the porch Uncle Morton began singing "What a friend we have in Jesus." One by one he was joined and soon a choir had formed on the porch. The sound of the voices and faith was so peaceful. The crickets and tree frogs seemed to join in. They sang hymn after hymn and even threw in a couple of verses from "The Twist" before they finished.

It was getting late and everyone thanked Clayton and Monie for having everyone over. Pastor White said he truly was glad he came. "I really enjoyed that there was no fighting."

Everyone laughed and we all headed for our cars and trucks.

"I'll see you all tomorrow at church," Uncle Morton said.

I went to bed and thought of holding Susie's hand in the full moon.

SUNDAY, JULY 10

We rode to church with Robert and Janice and James Ernest jumped in at the last moment. The sun was hidden behind clouds and Robert said he thought we would get rain soon. I knew it hadn't rained since I had arrived and that was over a month ago. Farmers were complaining about there crops. Monie had told Mamaw that her garden was suffering. The pastor began service asking God to give us rain. As he prayed we heard thunder outside and *Amen* was shouted around the room as he prayed. We could hardly hear the end of the prayer for the noise of the raindrops as they pelted the church's old tin roof.

As if planned with God, Pastor White preached on Noah's Ark. It was the most interesting sermon I had ever heard preached. Before he started the sermon he had all the young kids come up and he told them about all the animals that were escorted onto the Ark. He gave each child an animal that they were suppose to be during the sermon. He told them that when he mentioned their animal they were to make the animal sound real loud. He had a lion, duck, dog, cat, cow, bear, elephant and others. Bobby Lee wanted to be the dog. He had them practice their animal sound and then sent them back to their seat. If he just said *animals* they were all suppose to sound out. All the kids and adults were so attentive waiting to hear the next animal sound. When he said dog, Bobby Lee stood up in the pew and barked his head off.

The kids loved the interaction, except for Delma. She got stuck with the monkey and had to do the monkey sound and was not real happy about it as everyone laughed. In the end though, she seemed okay with it. When he said the ark finally landed on dry land and the animals got off the boat, the place sounded like a zoo.

At the end of the sermon he announced that the Wednesday kid's night would go on as planned. He apologized for what happened and said he had written apologies to each parent that had a child there.

The rain grew steady and it rained all afternoon. James Ernest ate dinner with us and spent the afternoon with me. We played games and watched some television. I told him about holding Susie's hand the night before.

I asked him, "Have you seen Sadie since Wednesday?"

"No. They're still grounded. I guess we'll see them when we see them. Mr. Tuttle was really mad about it."

"We could walk up there tomorrow and see if they're still alive." We both laughed.

We went out to the front porch. Papaw, Leo, and Coty were sitting on the porch. Coty came to me. He jumped up and put his front paws on me. I plopped down on the porch steps and played with him. The rain was still falling. The coolness of the

"I want to invite James Ernest and Uncle Morton, which would make six of us."

"That's perfect. You had better call and ask them to come. Tell Uncle Morton and Susie that Martin will pick them up around six."

I called everyone and they accepted my invitation.

That evening Coty and I went with Papaw to pick them up. We picked up Susie first. I noticed that Susie had a small present with her. The twins ran out and handed me a birthday card and asked me not to open it until later. Papaw then drove to Uncle Morton's house. I helped him into the cab. Morton was carrying a long burlap bag. Susie, Coty, and I jumped into the bed of the pickup. Pastor White came out the front door and wished me a happy birthday.

"Thank you. I enjoyed kid's night again last night."

"Me too," Susie shouted as Papaw drove away. When we returned to the house James Ernest was sitting on the porch petting Leo. Mamaw said supper would be ready soon. We all sat on the porch and talked.

"I hear the big hiking trip is this Monday. You should have good weather for it," Uncle Morton said.

"Should be just about perfect," Papaw added.

"I'm really excited about it. It should be a lot of fun."

"I want a full report on all the birds and animals that you see. Take a journal and write them down if you have to," Uncle Morton suggested.

"Okay." It actually didn't sound like a bad idea. Although I knew that I wouldn't know every bird that I saw.

Mamaw soon came out and said supper was ready and we all headed for the kitchen. I sat between Susie and Uncle Morton.

Papaw said grace and we dug into the fried chicken, mashed potatoes and green beans. We had cornbread with honey and sweet butter. Mamaw opened a jar of canned sweet pickles. They were so good. Everyone ate some of everything on the table. For dessert, Mamaw had made a coconut cake and of course cherry dumplings.

As we were eating dessert Mamaw placed a present in front of me on the table. I quickly tore into it throwing paper everywhere. Inside the box were new hiking boots. They were the coolest shoes I had ever seen.

"Thanks, I love them."

Uncle Morton asked Mamaw to give me the burlap bag. He said, "Since James Ernest is having a birthday soon also, I put a gift in there for both of you."

I untied the string from the top of the bag and had James Ernest slid the bag down and it exposed two carved hiking sticks. They were carved from hickory and had an animal carved into the top of each stick. One had a Red-tailed Hawk perched on top and the other had a coyote howling to the sky. Both were incredible. "They're fantastic, Uncle Morton."

"They're beautiful. Thank you," James Ernest said. "Did you carve these?"

"Yes. I don't have a lot else to do. Thought you boys would like them for your trip."

"We love them," I said.

"Which one belongs to me?" James Ernest asked.

"You two can decide that. It doesn't matter to me."

"It's your birthday, Timmy, you pick whichever one you want," James Ernest said.

"If you don't mind, I would like the Red-tailed Hawk."

18 THE BUTTERFLY FIELD

I had trouble sleeping. I was anticipating the morning light and the beginning to the hike with the Wolf Pack. Yesterday evening James Ernest and I took all of our supplies up the Tuttle's house and put them on the back porch. Papaw was going to take us up to the farm first thing this morning so we could start our trip.

I did all my chores yesterday afternoon. I mowed the grass and got fresh water from the spring. I cleaned up the path around the lake and swept off the front porch. I saw Susie at church yesterday morning and she wished us a good trip and said she would miss me. I'm not sure why. Normally we don't see each other but every few days anyway.

James Ernest showed up yesterday with a handmade backpack. He had taken branches and grapevines and formed a pack skeleton and then took a burlap bag and cut it and sewed it to size where it fit perfectly into the skeleton pack. He had found some old leather and made straps that he attached to form around his shoulders and waist to hold the pack on his back.

It looked a hundred years old, but it was one of the neatest things I had ever seen. He said he had been working on it since our trip to West Liberty to buy supplies. I would have never thought of making my own backpack.

James Ernest was at my bedroom window at the first sign of light. He climbed through headfirst and said, "I'm ready. I've never been so excited. Get up."

"I'm up." I flipped the sheet off and laid there with all my clothes already on. James Ernest laughed at me.

"Did you wear those to bed?"

"No. I couldn't sleep so I got up, got dressed and then laid back down. What time is it?"

"Five-thirty."

"I don't even think Mamaw is up fixing breakfast yet?" I could hear Coty outside my window whimpering. I got out of bed and walked over to the window and looked down at him. He sat there looking up at me with his tail going a mile a minute. "We'll be out in a little bit, Coty." A week ago Papaw decided it was time for Coty to start staying outside at night instead of by my bed.

Papaw had made him a doghouse and placed it close to Leo's. Coty wasn't happy about it at all. He slept outside my window the first two nights. The third night Papaw tied him to his doghouse for the night so he would get use to it. He now slept in it, but always showed up at daybreak below my window.

"I'm so ready to go that I couldn't sleep last night. I don't know if I slept at all. I don't think I've ever looked forward to something this much."

"Yeah. Me too," I said as I hopped out of bed and into my shoes. I saw the cross necklace hanging on the bedpost. I grabbed it and placed it quickly over my head.

I climbed out the window and James Ernest followed me. Coty began jumping up on me and I took time to greet him and pet him and scratch behind his ears. "It looks like Coty is excited about the trip also."

I walked over to a bush and peed. Coty peed against the bush next to us.

"What time are we supposed to be at the Tuttle's place?" James Ernest asked.

"Around seven."

The back door opened and Mamaw walked out onto the back porch.

"Good morning," I said.

Mamaw was startled and said, "You're going to make me pee before I make it to the outhouse. What are you boys doing out here so early?"

"We're anxious to get going on our trip."

"Not before you eat a good breakfast you're not," she demanded as she continued her walk to the outhouse. "I still can't believe they're letting you boys tramp off into the forest overnight. I can't believe it." She muttered as she closed the half-moon door.

I couldn't believe it either really. When we first came up with the idea I didn't think it would ever happen.

Mamaw fixed eggs and bacon, sausage, toast with honey, and pancakes. We drank orange juice and James Ernest had a large glass of milk. I gave Coty and Leo some leftover pancakes and bacon. Papaw had given me two cans of dog food to feed Coty during the hike.

At six-forty I asked Papaw if he could take us on up to the farm. We were all ready and wanted to get started. I went to my room and grabbed my Christmas binoculars from off the nightstand and checked my pocket for my knife and headed for the pickup.

James Ernest had made an extra copy of the trail map to give to Papaw in case they needed to come looking for us, at Papaw's insistence. It was probably a good idea. When we arrived at the farm, Randy was waiting on the porch with Sadie and Francis. They ran to the truck as it came to a stop. Randy was yelling, "Let's go! Let's go!" Coty jumped out of the bed and howled from all the commotion.

Papaw smiled and said, "They look ready."

"They sure do." Randy and Coty's excitement made me even more so.

I jumped out of the pickup and asked, "Where's Purty?"

"Still feeding his face. He thinks you guys are going to starve, so he's loading up on all the food he can stuff in his mouth," Sadie answered.

"I think he's trying to eat enough to last the two days," Randy said.

Forest and Loraine walked out onto the front porch and waved. "It's a good day for a hike in the woods. I wish I was going along," Forest proclaimed.

"It does make a fellow want to walk off into those woods doesn't it?" Papaw said.

"If you join the Wolf Pack you can go. The initiation is pretty bad though," James Ernest said.

Forest laughed and said, "No thanks."

Papaw just laughed.

Purty finally walked through the door. He looked like he could just barely walk.

"You okay?" I asked.

"Sure I am. Just a little stuffed."

Everyone headed to the back porch where all our gear was stored. We quickly began putting on our backpacks and checking our list. Everything checked out okay. Loraine gave everyone hugs including James Ernest and me. She then arranged us in a group and took plenty of pictures. She had us position ourselves differently for each picture. Coty sat in front looking at Papaw and the camera. Papaw said we looked like Daniel Boone and his men heading for the trails unknown. She then hugged us again and we quickly took off. Sadie said she was going to walk with us to the edge of the woods. Coty led the way. James Ernest and I had our walking sticks. Randy and Purty had sticks they had made themselves. Everyone waved and Sadie walked beside James Ernest and then gave him a kiss as we entered the woods. The other three of us made kissy sounds as she kissed him goodbye and continued even after Sadie had turned to head back home.

"Here we are guys," Randy said. He had us stand in our circle and howl to the sky like wolves. We then jumped up and down five times chanting, "Wolf Pack, Wolf Pack, Wolf Pack, Wolf Pack, Wolf Pack." We then held out our hands in the middle and we yelled, "Forever the Pack."

"The hike has officially begun," Randy proclaimed.

"I can't believe we're finally doing this," Purty said.

"Two days of hiking—just us," I agreed. Randy and James Ernest nodded in agreement.

"Does anyone's pack feel too heavy?" Randy asked.

Everyone said they were great. No problem. Purty asked, "How long will it take to get to our camping spot?"

"Papaw looked at the map that James Ernest gave him, and he thought it might be around ten miles to the camping spot."

"How long will that take?" Purty asked again.

I looked at James Ernest and Purty looked at Randy. "I guess we could walk two or three miles an hour. So it would take us three to five hours with no stops," Randy figured.

"Yeah, but we'll probably stop and rest quite a bit," James Ernest said.

Purty happily suggested, "Then we'll have plenty of time to explore and goof off. Maybe go swimming to cool off."

Everyone agreed. "We want to make sure we get to camp with plenty of daylight left so we can make camp though," James Ernest warned.

Randy quickly said he was right. I had on jean shorts and a t-shirt and a ball cap. I had on my new hiking boots that I had gotten for my birthday. I was carrying some of the food in my pack and a clean t-shirt and socks. Mamaw also made me take clean underwear. I had my walking stick and my new binoculars and necklace hanging around my neck. I also had a canteen around my neck. Mr. Tuttle had bought canteens for each of us. I had a small pad in my back pocket and a pen in my front pocket to write down all the birds I'd see for Uncle Morton.

Randy had a lantern in his backpack and had tied the tent to the bottom of his pack. James Ernest had a couple of sheets and the hatchet and some of the food in his pack. James Ernest was the only one that wore long pants. He had on bib jean overalls with a t-shirt underneath.

Purty had most of our food and his extra clothes in his backpack. Randy and Purty both had on hiking boots. James Ernest had on black high top tennis shoes. We all had on smiles as we walked down the trail. James Ernest began whistling and Purty recognized the song and started singing *Zip-a-dee-doo-dah, Zip-a-dee-ay*. Randy was laughing, but I couldn't keep from joining Purty in the singing. *My, oh my what a wonderful day! Plenty of sunshine heading my way.*

By now Randy and James Ernest jumped in and we all sang *Zip-a-dee-dah, zip-a -dee-ay*. Everyone laughed and Purty started skipping down the trail. Soon we all were skipping and singing again, *Mister Bluebird on my shoulder, it's the truth, it's actch'll, Everything is satisfactch'll, Zip-a-dee-dah, zip-a-dee-ay. Wonderful feeling, wonderful day!*

We continued singing until we came to the wide trail that led to the cabin. We turned west and headed toward the cabin. It was still early dawn and the sun had just risen to where we saw rays of sunshine on the trail. It was suppose to be a beautiful day. The high was going to be in the mid-eighties. I saw two Dark-eyed Juncos land on the trail ahead of us and I took out my pad and wrote it down. I also wrote down a sparrow and cardinal knowing that they were common and we would see plenty of them on our hike.

Coty ran toward the juncos, but they flew away seconds before he got to them. Then he was off again as something moved in the woods. I asked Randy and Purty, "What is it like to have so many brothers and sisters? Do you enjoy it? I think it would be fun."

"It's good and bad. There's always something going on. There is usually always laughter in the house, especially with Todd and Francis around. Billy is a real cut-up also. But it's hard to get time alone. You know, when a guy just wants time by himself to think and plan."

"All you ever plan is how to see Brenda more," Purty chimed in.

"You don't know anything."

"I know you like her and you want to kiss her." We all laughed.

"It's better than kissing your pillow like you were the other night."

Purty's eyes opened wide and he said, "But that pillow can be anyone I want her to be."

"Like who?" I asked

"I don't know, anyone, a movie star, a famous singer, Shirley Temple."

"Shirley Temple!"

"She's a little girl," Randy yelled.

"She's cute. She's older in her last movies."

"Your pillow is still kinda weird. You should use a Barbie doll," James Ernest said. We all laughed.

"Is that what you do?" Purty shot back.

James Ernest laughing said, "No, your sister." We all laughed at that.

"I like our big family. It's fun. What is it like being an only child?" Purty asked.

James Ernest took a moment before answering. "I guess I don't really like it. It's always lonely. Maybe that's why I like school. Sound, I like hearing sound going on."

"What about your mom? Doesn't she talk to you?" Randy asked.

"No. Not unless she's complaining about something I didn't do. Dad's not around any longer. Mom is shut up in her own little world. Sometimes I think she should be locked up in a looney bin."

"What's wrong with her?" I asked.

"I don't know. I think she just gave up after Dad left for good. It probably didn't help when I stopped talking. Some of it is probably my fault. She sits and stares out the window for hours at a time. I've asked her what she's thinking about," he hesitated and continued, "but she just says she's lost in a dream."

"We all do that, don't we? I do that in school," Randy offered. I realized that he was right. I was always daydreaming in school, not even hearing the sounds of the teacher or the other kids, thinking about the hot Kentucky summers, or Susie, or my grandparents. I might even be in the cave or being chased by the Tattoo Man. It actually didn't take much for me to get lost in thought.

"Yeah. I do it all the time. It doesn't mean I'm crazy. I think." I looked up and saw that the cabin was right in front of us and I could still imagine the rag bed in the corner and suddenly I felt something on my leg. I looked down, but nothing was there.

"Let's take a break. I need to relieve myself," Purty suggested. He threw his backpack and hiking stick down and took off for the woods. We walked to the fire pit and I dropped to one of the seats and rested. The pack wasn't really heavy, but it was uncomfortable after a while. I saw a Yellow-throated Warbler in a bush in the clearing and took out my pad and wrote it down. Coty was lying at my feet resting.

Soon we heard Purty say, "Boy that felt good. That was one big ol' poop."

I looked at him and asked, "What did you use for paper? I've got the toilet paper in my pack."

"I just used some leafs off a bush. It was fine."

We just shook our heads at him. We got up to continue the hike. We walked around the cabin and began on the trail north. "Has anyone ever been on this trail," I asked. Everyone answered, "No."

The trail was fairly narrow. We walked in single file. Weeds grew along the path, some reaching up to our waists. We could see that the woods were heavy with brush and undergrowth. Large trees canopied over the trail making it darker than the trail we had left behind. At times the only way I knew Coty was up ahead was the movement of the tall grasses. We walked silently for a while. It was nice listening to the sounds of the forest and the birds and squirrels chattering back and forth to each other.

I thought about James Ernest and his home life as we walked. We had things in common. Except, I had my mom who was always there for me, and I had a sister that I loved. We also had lived in a trailer at different times. We lived in trailer parks though, with our neighbors living fifteen feet from us. I didn't like trailer homes much.

After an hour and a half we came to a field covered with flowers and tall green grass. It was probably around an acre of ground. Butterflies were everywhere moving from plant to plant. I saw bluebirds flying over the field catching insects in their mouths. Chickadees flew back and forth across the meadow. I stopped to write them down. All the guys paused and watched the sight. It was really beautiful.

"Isn't this purty? One of the purtiest things I've ever seen," Purty exclaimed.

"You're right," said Randy.

Coty was chasing butterflies and James Ernest walked over to get a closer look at one of the flowers. I had no idea what kinds of flowers were there. It seemed as though all the colors of the world was in that one field.

"It really is pretty, Purty," I agreed.

Randy suddenly raised his arms to get our attention.

"Quiet. Look over there." A herd of deer stood at the far end of the field. I counted eleven. James Ernest said he counted twelve. Six were fawns and they were leaping and chasing each other around the field. The mothers had noticed us and were keeping their eyes on us. We stood motionless and I looked to see where Coty was. He was still chasing butterflies. He was so small that he couldn't see over the grasses to see the deer.

We dropped our backpacks and I put the binoculars to my eyes and watched the fawns play in the meadow. Every once in a while a mothers white tail would rise. I passed the glasses to everyone else, and we took turns watching the deer. This was the most deer I had ever seen together in my life, and I wanted to take it all in while I had the chance. Overhead I saw a large bird flying above the meadow. I looked at James Ernest and pointed toward it. He whispered that it was a Red-shouldered Hawk. I wrote it down. The hawk began a downward flight. I motioned for everyone to look. The hawk soon swooped a few feet above the flowers and grabbed one of the smaller birds that were busy catching flying insects.

"Wow! Did you see that?" I said excitedly.

The hawk then flew away with the bird in his talons and landed in a tall pine at the edge of the field. Randy watched the hawk through my binoculars.

"He's ripping the bird apart and eating it."

"Let me see," Purty begged.

We took turns watching the hawk destroy the bird. I looked back to the deer, but they were no longer there. We may have scared them away, or maybe the hawk did.

I needed a drink of water and took my first sip out of the canteen. The others followed my lead. The canteens were a good idea.

Coty ran up to me with a stick in his mouth. He seemed so excited. It was as if he had captured it and wanted to show me his great possession. I poured some water into my hand and he slurped at it. I could tell he wanted more. I filled my hand with water again for him. We decided we had better be going, so we gathered our stuff and headed on down the trail.

19 ESCAPED BEARLY

MONDAY, JULY 25

We hiked and talked about the meadow and all the neat things we had seen. The woods around us became less dense. The underbrush had been replaced with moss covered tree trunks, large rocks and small saplings trying to survive the dominance of the large oaks and pines that filled the forest floor.

We could see deep into the forest and we all spent time looking for movement as we walked along the wider trail. We now walked two-by-two. I walked beside Purty. Randy and James Ernest led the way.

Purty looked at me and said, "I wish I could hike with no clothes on."

"Why? Why would you want to do that?"

"I feel trapped in these clothes. Like I want to escape and be free."

"I think you would get all bit up with bug bites, and you would get scratches all over your body." I thought about it and then said, "In places where you wouldn't want to get scratches. The backpack would rub against your skin."

"You may be right, but I love walking around nude."

"Don't you care about people seeing you naked?" I asked.

"Nah. It's just skin. Just like my arm. Parts of our bodies are shaped different, but it's still just skin."

"Okay." I thought for a second and then added, "But remember when Randy told us about seeing your aunt naked?"

"Yeah."

"Why did you ask Randy when your aunt was visiting again if she just has skin like we do? You wanted to see her naked."

Purty studied on it for a while and then answered, "I guess you got me on that one. Do you think it's wrong for me to walk around naked?"

"Not around us guys. We don't care. I do think it's a bit weird. But I figure it's wrong to walk around in front of girls without your clothes."

Purty laughed and said, "You just think the girls will like me better than you."

He pushed me on my shoulder and I almost fell over. Randy and James Ernest looked back at us and smiled. They made some comment that I couldn't hear.

We walked on for a couple of minutes and I said, "If you were married to a beautiful woman that you loved very much, would you like it if she decided to walk around nude in front of all your friends?"

"I guess I never thought that much about it. I just always enjoyed being naked. You're probably right, I wouldn't like it. "

"Well, if you marry a beautiful woman and decide you don't care, you'll probably have a lot of friends." Purty looked puzzled, and then it dawned on him what I meant, and he laughed.

"Yep."

I could see that the trail ended ahead of us. We hurried to catch up with the others. As we got to them we came upon a wide shallow creek flowing east. It was filled with rocks and large boulders creating small waterfalls and eddies everywhere.

"Isn't that purty?" Coty wandered over and drank from the creek and walked into a little pool and sat in it. We laughed at him.

"Maybe we can find a pool to swim in later like Coty," I suggested.

Randy chipped in, "According to the map we turn left here and follow upstream for a few miles. We should find a good coolin' off spot somewhere this afternoon. We can cool off then."

James Ernest told us, "By the map, the Big Butt Rock is 'bout half way up the creek."

"Oh, boy!" Purty said excitedly.

We turned upstream, and I yelled for Coty, and he came running and shaking off the water. The trail was slightly uphill and rocky. The trail we left was smooth and flat. This was totally different, and I had to keep my eyes on my footsteps as I walked - to keep from tripping. Purty had almost fallen twice already. It was already eleven and according to the map we were only about a third of the way to the camping spot and the first third was easy walking. We had spent almost an hour at the meadow watching everything.

Purty wanted to lead the way for a while. I think he wanted to be the first one to spot the Big Butt Rock. I brought up the rear again as we walked on the single-file wide path. We had to maneuver around trees and large trunks and at certain spots we climbed over fallen trees. Randy was right in front of me. I kept an eye on the creek as we moved along. It was pretty.

The sun was high in the sky and shining on us now. It wasn't real hot, but it felt hot due to the hiking that we were doing. My t-shirt was soaked with sweat, especially where the pack was hanging on my back. I could see beads of sweat on Randy's neck. I took another long drink from my canteen. I was hoping we would stop soon for lunch and rest, but we kept hiking.

I caught a glimpse of movement out of the corner of my eye. I looked toward the water and quickly stopped and picked up a rock and threw it at Randy. He turned around. I put my finger to my mouth signaling him to be quiet. I pointed to the other side of the water. He threw a rock at James Ernest and did the same. They slowly walked back to where I was. We hid behind two large trees along the water edge and watched a black bear walk along the tree line on the other side of the creek. It looked like she had found a berry patch. Soon I noticed two cubs come out of the thicket into the clearing. They hopped around and bounded over the rocks and followed their mother to the water. They all got drinks from the water.

"Where's Purty?" I asked.

"He took off and left us. He's trying to get to the rock. We'd better be careful. A mother bear isn't very friendly, especially when her cubs are around," James Ernest explained.

"What should we do?" I asked quietly.

"Let's stay put. Do you think she has seen us?"

"I don't think so. She hasn't looked toward us," I whispered.

Suddenly Coty barked. The sound came from up the trail. The bear raised her head and looked across the creek toward the sound. I also looked toward the bark to find Coty. I had hoped Coty would continue toward Purty. We were probably fifty to eighty feet away from the cubs and their mother now seemed a lot more concerned. The cubs began wrestling in the water.

Coty barked again and then again. He must have been chasing a squirrel or something else in the forest. I now saw Coty bouncing back down the trail at us. He acted like we were playing hide-and-seek and he got excited seeing us and began barking again. The bear stood on her hind legs and moved forward toward him. It startled me as to how big the bear was when she stood. The bear growled and Coty turned toward her. He saw the bear across the creek and growled back.

I was trying to whisper, *"No Coty, No."* But Coty couldn't hear me. Coty ran to the edge of the water and continued barking and growling at the mother. He then saw the cubs and turned his attention to them.

I looked at James Ernest and asked, "What do we do? Coty will get killed. I have to do something." I was worried about Coty getting killed, but I had never considered that we might actually get killed. It had seemed exciting and fun watching the bears, but now it was serious. The bear was moving closer to Coty.

James Ernest looked at me as though he was thinking and finally said, "Wait, and follow me when I go."

He took off his canteen and slid it into my backpack. James Ernest slowly slid his body down the tree. He crawled forward to where some rocks were. He picked up a large rock and threw it over his body and across the creek. It landed behind the mother bear with a loud thud. The bear quickly turned away toward the sound and James Ernest got up and ran toward Coty motioning for us to follow. He rapidly bent down and scooped up Coty as he ran with us on his heels. I glanced toward the bear; she had turned back and was standing again and growling at us. She ran halfway across the creek but stopped as we disappeared over a rise in the trail.

We ran as long as we could with backpacks on. We could

see the trail for quite a ways behind us and there was no sign of the bears. We stopped and tried to catch our breaths.

"Good plan," I gasped.

"That was exciting," Randy said.

"It was more than exciting, it was scary. That's the first time I've ever seen a bear in the wild," I said.

James Ernest was still holding Coty. Coty was giving him dog kisses on his face. "I think he appreciates you saving him," Randy said.

"I appreciate it too," I said.

James Ernest laughed and said, "Okay, but don't give me any kisses."

"Wasn't planning on it, but thanks."

We decided we should carry Coty for a little ways. Sometimes I would forget that he was still a puppy. It was amazing watching him growl at the bears. He was taking his stand. I knew then he would grow up to be a great dog, if he didn't get killed first.

"I think I've seen that bear before," James Ernest said.

"What?"

"When?"

"Last fall, I was walking up Morgan Road toward the quarry, and she walked across the road about a hundred yards ahead of me. She saw me, but continued across the road to Licking Creek. I walked up there and watched her for a little while until she disappeared into the forest.

"Why did you never tell me?" I asked.

"Forgot about it. We never talk about bears."

"I didn't even know there were bears in this area," Randy said.

"Me either."

"There must be at least two adults around," James Ernest reasoned.

"How do you know?" I asked.

"Well, how do you think she had babies? There has to be a daddy bear somewhere."

I acted like I knew all about the reproduction of bears and said, "Oh yeah, you are probably right."

Randy tapped me on the head and asked, "Probably?" He and James Ernest laughed. I wasn't sure what they were laughing about, but I joined in.

"I can't believe Todd missed seeing the bears," Randy said.

"He won't believe us when we tell him," I said as we walked on up the trail. James Ernest decided to let Coty down and he squatted and pooped just off the trail.

"It just about scared the poop out of me too," James Ernest teased.

Randy and I agreed.

It was unbelievable how much we had seen in just over five hours. We talked about the hike already being a success without anything else needing to happen. I looked forward to getting back and telling Susie about the bears, the meadow, and the butterflies. We walked in silence for the next half hour. I listened to the sounds of the forest and the sounds of the babbling stream beside us. The wet moss-covered rocks glistened in the sun. The trail continued moving uphill and the climb was becoming tiring. I was ready for a break when we heard Purty yell out, "Hey, guys, over here."

We looked over to the other side of the creek and there was the Big Butt Rock, and Purty was bent over next to it—mooning us. They looked just alike except the rock was a hundred times bigger. It was astonishing. It did look just like a big old butt. It wasn't two rocks side by side like I thought it would be. It was one big boulder in the shape of what it was named after. There was no mistaking it. The sight of Purty bent over next to it was too funny. We dropped our packs and took off our shoes and waded over to it.

"Isn't it great?" Purty said as though he had just discovered an eighth wonder of the world. And he probably thought it was.

We all felt it and looked it over. "I dare you guys to kiss it," Randy challenged us.

"I'm not kissing the Big Butt," I quickly said.

James Ernest laughed and said, "It's just a rock."

"I don't care; it's the idea of it."

"I'll kiss it," Purty yelled.

Randy shouted to him, "You'd marry the thing. You are one weirdo."

"Let's eat lunch," James Ernest suggested.

Everyone liked that idea. We walked back to our packs. Randy asked Purty to put his clothes back on so the sight of his body wouldn't ruin our lunch. He got dressed as we dug in his pack looking for the food. James Ernest and I were pulling out the cans and boxes. "What is this dark yucky stuff all over everything?" I asked.

James Ernest had the same stuff on his fingers. He smelled it and said, "It smells like chocolate." He licked it and said, "It is chocolate. Purty! Why is there chocolate on everything?"

"Oh man! The Hershey bars must have melted."

"Didn't Mom put them in a separate bag?" Randy asked.

"Yeah, but I thought they would melt in a bag so I took them out and took the brown covers off of them. I thought it would keep them from melting."

Randy shook his head and said, "What did you think they would do in a backpack in eighty-five degree heat. It's probably a hundred in the pack."

"Guess I figured wrong." All the food in his pack was covered in melted chocolate. He had to wash or lick off everything that was in his pack. His extra clothes were covered in Hershey chocolate.

"First time I've had chocolate-covered sardines," James Ernest said as he opened the sardine can. He took a couple and passed them around. The crackers were passed around also. We ate sardines and saltine crackers and drank our water from the canteens. I gave Coty a couple of sardines. We each had a banana flip for dessert.

Finally Randy said, "You'd never guess what you missed about a mile back."

"You mean the bear," Purty calmly said.

The three of us looked at each other bewildered. "How did you know that?" Randy asked.

"I saw it when I walked past it. It was eating raspberries. Two cubs were heading into the woods."

"You saw them and didn't stop to watch them?" I asked.

"No. I wanted to find the Big Butt Rock."

Randy picked up a pebble and threw it at Purty. James Ernest and I followed Randy's example. Soon Purty was being showered with small pebbles and anything else we could find. When we finished he looked up and said, "They were purty though, especially the little ones."

We told him about how James Ernest had saved Coty. "Sounds like you bearly escaped," Purty said through his grin.

We tackled him.

Randy said, "We have to hurry if we're going to make it to the camp by nightfall."

Purty asked, "Couldn't we just camp anywhere?"

"We could if there's somewhere to pitch a tent and build a fire."

James Ernest chipped in, "We don't know anything about the next trail. Randy is right, we had better not fool around."

Once we got to the top, it was only a couple hundred yards to the turn off. There was no sign, but it was easy to see.

It wasn't long before we could no longer hear the water cascade over the cliff and the trail narrowed to no more than a deer route. We were hiking through deep forest with heavy treetops blocking out any light from the sun. It was only seven-thirty and still two hours before dark, but we were on the east side of the mountain and in seemed like dusk on the trail. Randy led the way, and he kept up a hurried pace as we climbed higher and higher up the mountainside.

Coty walked beside me. He even seemed tired and a little spooked by the closing in of the darkness. He stayed close by. We had filled our canteens before we left the creek, and I drunk from it often as we walked. Purty was walking in front of me. He was constantly itching his butt and scratched at his arms.

I asked him, "What's wrong with you Purty? Why do you keep scratching?"

"I don't know. I may have gotten some bug bites or something. I'm itching to death."

"You'd better keep up with Randy and James Ernest. We don't want to get too far behind them."

"I'm trying."

It was almost nine o'clock and we still hadn't reached the

top of the mountain where we guessed the campsite was. It was hard to see the trail. Randy and I both got out our flashlights to make sure we didn't stray from the small trail. The trail up the mountain was steep and there was no flat ground to pitch a tent. We had to keep going.

Coty stopped and looked at me in certain disgust. "Come on Coty. I promise it won't be much longer. Come on, boy." He followed after I gave him a drink. His poor tongue hung from the side of his mouth, and he breathed heavily with each step. After another fifteen minutes the trail leveled off, and I felt relived to be on flat ground.

"It should be right up here," Randy guessed.

"I sure hope so," Purty groaned.

An owl flew down the trail toward us and just over our head scaring all of us. We could hear howls in the distance and Whippoorwills in the forest. A few minutes later Randy called out, "We're here. We made it."

We were at a clearing and it looked like a possible bald on the mountain. We looked around for a fire pit but couldn't find one. James Ernest and I began putting up the tent while Randy went to look for firewood. Purty stood watching and scratching himself. "I think I'm dying here."

"What's wrong with Purty?" James Ernest asked.

"His butt itches real bad. And his arms," I answered.

James Ernest and I had practiced putting the tent up several times before the trip. It didn't take long to get it up. I held the flashlight as James Ernest was using the blunt end of the hatchet to drive the pegs into the ground. He asked Purty, "What kind of leaves did you use?"

"What do you mean?" he asked.

"When you went to the bathroom you said you used leaves. What kind?"

"I don't know. I just pulled off a couple of handfuls from a bush."

"I bet you used poison ivy leaves. That's why you're itching so badly," James Ernest explained.

"But it was a big bush."

"Sometimes they grow into big bushes."

"Oh man! I can't believe it," Purty moaned.

Randy asked, "What's wrong?" as he returned with an armful of sticks.

I explained, "James Ernest thinks Purty used poison ivy for toilet paper this morning. He's itching like crazy."

"You idiot! Why did you do that?" Randy didn't seem to have much sympathy for Purty's dilemma. "Let's look for some rocks to build a pit, and I'll get a fire started."

We each quickly found a couple of rocks. We laid them in a circle, and Randy began working on the fire. He said, "Over there I saw a couple of logs we could carry over to sit on."

"We'll get them," James Ernest said. I went with him and we made two trips with the logs. By the time we got back Randy had the fire going. Randy then took the lantern from his backpack and lit it. He hung it on a branch in a nearby tree and our campsite was pretty good to go.

I took out my knife and went to the same tree and cut off four small limbs and stripped the smaller branches from them. I brought them back and laid them near the fire.

"What are those for?" Purty asked.

"Marshmallows," I answered. "Mamaw sent them. She said we couldn't have a campfire without toasting marshmallows."

"Alright! Let's get the food out. I'm starving," Purty said.

We emptied the sticky food packages out and everyone grabbed what they wanted. It looked like a feeding frenzy. Randy warned, "Don't forget. We have breakfast and lunch tomorrow."

Randy and I opened a sleeve of crackers and a can of Spam and made sandwiches. Coty was very interested in the Spam, but I opened one of the cans of dog food for him and spread it out on a rock. He gobbled it down in no time and came looking for more. I figured he was probably as hungry as we were, and I gave him some spam. He didn't seem as happy with it, but he ate it after hesitating. Purty and James Ernest each opened a can of Vienna sausages and ate them with crackers.

Purty took bites between scratching. James Ernest finally said, "I think if you spread mud on the spots it will relive the itching."

"Really, but where am I going to find mud."

Randy shook his head and said, "You really are an idiot. Just dig up some dirt in front of you and pour some water on it, ta-da, instant mud!"

"Oh, yeah."

We watched Purty as he took one of the sticks and scraped a hole in the hard dirt. He took out all the pebbles. He tilted his canteen and poured water unto the loose dirt and mixed it all around. He then took off his pants and pulled down his white Hanes underwear and asked if someone would spread the mud on him.

We all looked at him like he was a leper.

Randy said, "You must be kidding."

He took the hint and grabbed himself a handful of mud

inside that can be applied to the rash and it helps it scab over and heal. We can break some off. It should relive the itching. In the fall you can eat the seeds and they taste like walnuts."

Purty was in the water washing and splashing. The dirt and mud was falling off of him as he splashed around in the water. He finished and got out and began shaking like a dog trying to get the water off. We didn't bring towels so we had to wait for him to dry by the morning air.

"Who's going to apply it to my butt?"

We all looked at each other. I could tell that James Ernest hadn't thought about that. No one volunteered very quickly. "Come on guys. I can't do it myself. It will stay between us guys, Wolf Pack promise."

James Ernest finally said, "I'll do it. It was my idea. Wolf Pack promise, right?" He looked at each of us and we shook our heads up and down.

He had Purty put on his shirt and socks and then lay down on his stomach on a nearby flat rock. He showed Randy and me how to break off the stems of the Jewelweed. He told Purty to scratch the rash really hard for a while trying to break the rash open. James Ernest then squeezed the liquid from the hollow stems and let it run all over the rash so that it covered it. He then told Purty to reach back and rub it in.

"Do you have clean clothes in your pack?"

"Yeah, except for the chocolate on them."

"That won't matter."

I went to his pack and went through it and found his shorts and underwear. They did have chocolate stains all over them. He quickly pulled them on. James Ernest then placed Jewelweed juice on Purty's arms and had him rub it in real good.

When he was done Purty looked at us and smiled. "It's working. It doesn't itch nearly as much."

"Try your best not to scratch it for a while. Let it dissolve into the rashes. It should really help."

"Why didn't we do this yesterday?" Purty asked.

"Jewelweed only grows along water and we weren't around water when I found out about it. According to the map I knew we would come to water again today, and I was hoping we would find Jewelweed for you."

"What about the mud? I thought it was suppose to work," Purty asked.

James Ernest smiled and said, "It relieved it for a while didn't it."

"Yeah."

"Well, it mainly was for us. I wanted to see if you would actually do it." We all began laughing except for Purty. "It was pretty funny watching you spread mud all over your butt and arms. I could hardly keep a straight face as you were digging ditches in your arms." I cracked up as James Ernest explained his trick. Purty just stood there with a stunned look on his face. He probably would have expected it from Randy or me, but not James Ernest.

He looked at James Ernest with a worried look on his face and asked, "So what will this Jewelweed juice stuff do on my butt. Attract bees and bears or something worse."

We were laughing so hard at the thought of bees swarming around him trying to fly into his pants toward the Jewelweed juice, or a bear attacking him to lick the juice away. After we stopped laughing so much James Ernest answered, "No. The magical Jewelweed is the real thing. I don't think anything is attracted to it. Not that I've read anyway."

"Makes me feel real secure, jerk."

We laughed again as we walked on down the trail. We would walk in silence and soon someone would begin laughing again. This went on for the next half hour.

The stream was *real purty*. Purty told us this several times and we had to agree. It was small, but it was so wild and colorful with the different summer flowers and trees reflecting in the small pools that formed along the rocks and tree roots that had stretched in to get a drink of the water.

This time we were walking down hill and it made the trail easier and the going faster. I hadn't seen Purty scratch one time since putting the Jewelweed on. We were walking due south. The sun was finally high enough to our left that we began feeling its warmth as we walked.

I remembered the Hanson ghost story and wondered if we would walk by the spot where he was murdered. Had we already walked by the spot? It always amazed me how people could be so mean and heartless to do the things they did - to steal from someone, or hurt someone, or even kill someone. There were so many good people and then a few that thought they could do whatever they wanted. But I wondered why did they want to do bad things.

My mind was on these things as I looked ahead to see the trail make a sharp turn to the left. The stream was continuing to the south. All of a sudden I heard a loud yelp. I heard crying and whimpering coming from the stream. I looked around for Coty, but I knew deep down that the sounds were coming from him. It sent a shiver through my body. I threw off my pack and ran toward the sound. Everyone else did the same as we ran toward the painful howling. As we ran toward him, the howling stopped.

I saw him lying in the stream.

"Coty! Coty!" I cried out. When we got over him we saw that his leg was caught in a steel trap. Blood was flowing down the stream. His big brown eyes looked up into my face and he cried. Randy and James Ernest carefully opened the trap, and I slowly pulled Coty from the metal contraption. I carried him toward the trail and laid him in the grass. My tears were falling into Coty's face. I looked around to see Randy throw the trap as far as he could and heard him cuss the trapper who had left it there.

Coty tried to lick his leg which I thought was a good sign. Dogs always licked their hurts and wounds. His leg looked pretty torn up. Blood seemed to be pouring from the wound. The teeth of the trap had dug deep into his leg. I didn't know if it was broken or not, but it was bleeding a lot. James Ernest tore his shirt off and made rags out of it and he tied a tourniquet above the wound. We then began wrapping his leg with the rags.

Purty asked between his sobs, "Would there be anything in the medicine kit that we could use?"

"Yeah, maybe."

Purty quickly looked through my pack, took the kit out and ran it back over to us. James Ernest carefully took the rags back off. He left the tourniquet on. Purty took out a tube and said, "Would antibiotic ointment be good?"

"Yeah."

He handed it to James Ernest and he squirted the whole

23 WHIRLING CIRCLES

When we made it to the farm field Sadie, Francis and Billy were running toward us. Sadie and Francis had tears in their eyes when they reached us.

"How is Coty?" Francis pleaded.

"Is he going to be okay?" Sadie asked.

"We don't know. Did they call Papaw?" I asked.

"Yeah. I think someone is coming."

Everyone was crowding around Coty as I continued to walk fast toward the house. I didn't want to run, because I didn't want to jar Coty's leg. Sadie grabbed one of James Ernest hands and held it tight. As we neared the back of the house Susie came through the backdoor and ran with tears flowing from her eyes. She stopped just short of me as I continued around the house and asked, "Is he okay?"

"I don't know." I began crying again after seeing the emotion pouring from her. "He's breathing, but I know he's hurting real bad."

"Is Papaw here?"

I heard Clayton answer the question, "He had went into town. Corie called and asked if I could take you to Dr. Green's office. Let's go."

"Thanks."

Susie and I jumped into the cab with Clayton. James Ernest and Sadie jumped into the back.

"Anyone else going," Clayton yelled. Francis climbed in the back also. Billy wanted to go, but Loraine said, "No way. You get back here." Loraine was on the front porch talking up a storm, but no one was listening as we hurriedly drove away from the house.

I yelled out the window, "Thanks, Randy." Randy was bent over with his hands on his knees. Billy stood there waving good-bye. I knew he was worn out and I knew Randy didn't want to go through watching Coty suffer. I learned a lot about the softness of Randy's heart and his willingness to help others.

Susie asked if she could hold Coty.

"I can't."

"It's okay. I understand," she said.

Clayton was driving as fast as he could and still be safe. He had three kids in the bed of the truck and didn't want to lose them going around a curve. We finally came to the lane that went to Dr. Green's veterinarian office. James Ernest jumped out of the truck before it stopped and ran into the office and before I got out of the cab, Dr. Green was out the door and meeting us.

"Follow me into the operating room."

We hurried into the room. Clayton, Francis, and Sadie stayed outside in the waiting room. I heard Sadie ask why Susie got to go inside and she didn't get to.

Dr Green began checking his breathing and heartbeat. He carefully took off the bandage. He asked what we had put on it.

"Antibiotic cream," James Ernest answered.

Dr. Green said, "You guys did a nice job. You did all you could have done. You may have saved his life."

"What do you mean *may have saved his life?*" I asked.

"Coty has lost a lot of blood. We'll start an IV and I'll stitch up the cuts. I'll need to get X-rays to see if there is any bone damage. I'll do everything I can. You know I will, Timmy."

"Please save him, Doc. Please!"

"Everyone needs to go to the waiting room so I can get started. You can stay out there or go home. I'll call you when I know something."

"I'm not leaving until I know something." I bent down and kissed Coty and said, "Live, Coty. We still have a lot of adventures to do together."

We all turned and walked out to the waiting room. I left the room with tears flowing. Papaw was there sitting with Clayton. I tried wiping them away and asked, "How did you know to come here?"

"Corie called the bank looking for me. I had just left the bank minutes earlier and went to the general store. She talked to Miss Simmons and she ran all over town until she found me. Here I am. How is Coty?"

We explained to everyone what Dr. Green said.

"What happened to him?" Papaw asked.

We explained how we heard him yelp and told them about finding him caught in the steel trap. We told them every detail about bandaging him and carrying him. We told how Randy ran so far to call.

Clayton said that some men still put out traps to catch mink in the streams. Papaw said that they didn't care about other animals getting caught.

"That's a cruel way to catch animals," Susie said.

Papaw and Clayton agreed with her.

We all waited for an hour. Dr. Green's assistant asked everyone that came in who needed the doctor to please come back if possible. She told them he was on an emergency. While we waited we talked about the hike. We told them about the butterfly field and the waterfall. We laughed out loud as we told them about Purty's poison ivy and how James Ernest had him spread mud on himself. We then told them about the bears.

Papaw said, "What? You saw bears."

We told them how Coty was barking at them and about how we escaped with Coty. Papaw just shook his head.

"I haven't heard of bears being around here for years," Clayton said. James Ernest told them about seeing one last year.

We then told them about the ghost and the graveyard. Papaw said that it was his grandfather's grave. He said his father was buried there, too. Papaw said he had heard the Hanson ghost story. Francis asked to hear the ghost story. James Ernest told her he would tell it to her around a campfire some night.

Finally Dr. Green came out to talk to us. He had a worried look on his face. Francis was first to ask, "Is he okay?"

"He does have a small bone fracture. But that can be fixed easily. He has lost a lot of blood, and as of now, I'm just not sure if he'll make it or not. I've stitched the cuts and done all that I can do for now. I know it's hard, but we'll just have to wait and see if he comes out of it," Doc Green explained. "If he wakes again, he'll be okay. He's just lost a lot of blood."

"I want to stay. I need to stay with him. Can I? Please."

"It's okay with me. I'm always around. I'll be around check-

24 RETURN TO THE BUTTERFLY FIELD

I awoke to the constant loud humming of the three large fans situated throughout the house. They were trying to relieve the heat that poured through the open windows and attempted to give us some hint of cooler breeze. It wasn't working. I felt as though circulated heat currents were blasting me over and over again. Again this morning my sheets were wet from sweat.

It had been the hottest first half of August on record, the weatherman said. Everyday the thermometer on the porch went well above a hundred. When a car drove by the store, the dust lingered in the air creating an unvarying cloud that engulfed the store. With the open windows and the fan blades sucking in the outside air it created a cloud-like effect inside the house. Clayton said that the crops were suffering and the ground was so hard it couldn't be worked. Everyone and everything seemed to be suffering.

Mamaw and Papaw bent their rule and decided that Coty could stay inside the house while he healed from his injury. Mamaw said that if Coty started to pee in the house that I had better be there to catch it. He laid stretched out on the wooden floor trying to soak in any coolness that was in it. He ignored the pillow by my bed that was placed there for him. During the past three weeks I had changed his bandage everyday and helped him do exercises to strengthen the leg. We went for walks around the lake in the early morning. The heat had kept away the fishermen. We had the lake all to ourselves. I took him to the Collins' swimming hole almost everyday and made him swim.

He still walked with a big limp. His muscles had been torn by the steel trap and they were slowly healing. Dr. Green said he might limp for the rest of his life. Coty seemed happy and glad to be alive. He even ran with a limp. The small fracture was pretty much healed, but his muscles were still trying to. I was thrilled that Coty had lived, and I knew he would be fine even if he did limp. Everyone adapts to the defects they're given. Uncle Morton is blind, I can't say every word correctly, and Coty limps. Big deal, we smile and live and laugh. I figured we had to accept our dents and count our blessings and be glad they weren't worse.

Uncle Morton had spent the evening with us a couple of days ago and I went over the list of birds that I saw on the hike. He asked all kinds of questions about each one. I answered what I could.

I laid in my own pool of sweat and thought about different imperfections and all my loved ones and friends who had them. I realized that one name didn't come up—Susie. I couldn't think of one wrong thing about her. Maybe she would think her freckles, but I liked them. To me the freckles weren't a dent. I knew she was perfect.

I would only see the Tuttle kids once in a while in the evenings. They did their chores in the early mornings and hid in the house during the heat of the day. James Ernest would spend afternoons with me. We would play cards and games and play with Coty. We drank a lot of soda pop.

Susie was coming down this afternoon and we were going to take Coty to the swimming hole. Pastor White held Sunday services earlier due to the heat. Yesterday it started at eight in the morning and everyone appreciated beating the heat. Wednesday kids' night had been cancelled the last two weeks.

Janice Easterling and the other women had been getting ready for the wedding, which was less than two weeks away now. They were also trying to finish a wedding quilt that they had been working on to give them as a gift. Dana and Idell walked around with nervous grins on their faces as the date drew near. Everyone teased them; the men were always reminding Dana about the old ball-and-chain.

"You ignore those old fools; they wouldn't know what to do without us women. They would walk around in filthy clothes and then starve to death," Ruby told Dana. The other women said, "Amen."

Purty's poison ivy cleared up fairly fast. Mrs. Tuttle said she had never heard of Jewelweed and was as impressed with James Ernest as we were. Sadie told her mom that *her* James Ernest was the smartest boy alive.

Mamaw called out that breakfast was ready. She had been fixing big meals for breakfast and had told us that we had better eat up, because she wouldn't be cooking any more in the heat. It made sense. We ate big in the mornings and had sandwiches the rest of the day. When I walked into the kitchen I saw that we were having eggs, sausage, biscuits and gravy, and pancakes. I loved Mamaw's sausage gravy. She used hot sausage in it, and it was perfect.

I let Coty out the back door and he limped away to do his business. We ate heartily and talked about the plans for the day. Mamaw asked, "Could you go get a bucket of water for me at the spring?"

"Sure. I'll go as soon as I'm done eating."

I ate and went to gather the water at the spring. Coty went with me and walked by my side. Trucks from the quarry would cover us with dust as they drove by. The dust would just hang in the air. There was no air to move it away. When we returned, Papaw took Coty and me to West Liberty with him. We went to the bank. I went in to say hello to Mr. Harney and Miss Rebecca. We then took Coty for his check-up with Dr. Green. Dr. Green thought Coty was doing great for what he had gone through. When we returned from town, Susie was waiting for me on the porch. Monie, Ruby and Janice were there quilting with Mamaw. Coty walked in and greeted everyone as if he owned the place.

Monie said, "He's looking pretty good. I'm glad."

Janice agreed and said, "Timmy, what are you doing with Coty when you have to go back home?"

I hadn't thought about it much. I had been concerned with him healing and not about his future. "I don't guess I know."

"Robert asked me to tell you that Coty could stay with us. I think Robert has grown fond of the little guy."

Monie interrupted, "Clayton thought he would do well at our farm. He would have plenty of kids for him to play with." Susie beamed with excitement.

Ruby quickly added, "I think Homer and I put in first claims for the pup a long time ago."

"Wait a darn minute. Martin and I have never said Coty

couldn't stay right here at his home," Mamaw spoke up. Everyone started talking at the same time. They were arguing about who should have Coty. No one was listening to anyone else. They were all too busy stating their cases for him. Susie and I quietly left through the back door, took Coty with us, and headed to the swimming hole.

"I guess Coty will have a home."

Susie laughed and I said, "Unless they kill each other over him."

"Who do you want Coty to stay with?"

"Myself. I can't stand the thought of having to leave him. I want him with me. I think he would miss me."

"There's no doubt he would."

"I guess he would like to stay at the store, since that's his home. Though he would probably like being with you on the farm."

"I think he would. I would take real good care of him."

"I know. He could play with the goats and Mr. Perry and chase the chickens." I thought about it and added, "It's a big decision. I'll have to think about it some more. It's between you and Mamaw and Papaw." I knew that Coty would probably like staying at the store where he was at home, but I also knew Coty would like to have kids to play with and other animals around. I had two weeks to decide.

We jumped into the water and it felt so good in the stifling heat. Coty jumped in and began swimming around with us. We played with Coty in the pool until he got too tired to swim anymore. He went under a tree and fell asleep in the shade. Susie and I decided to swim into the Indian cave. We knew it would be nice and cool inside.

We were right. It felt so great; we didn't want to go back out to the afternoon heat. We couldn't stay long though. I was afraid Coty would wake and wonder where we were. I wished I would have taken Coty back to house before we swam inside.

Susie asked, "Will you take me to the butterfly field as soon as the heat breaks?"

"Sure. You'll love it."

"I'm sure I will. But I don't know if this heat will ever quit though."

The Masons had a picnic last weekend and two of the men died from heat-stroke during the festivities. The paper had a story about it, and it was on the local television newscast. Mamaw had seen the report, huffed and said, "Bunch of stupid men. It seems God didn't favor them with much sense."

We spent around a half hour in the cave before we decided that we needed to go back out to Coty. Susie led the way and we swam out through the opening and into the pool. When we popped out of the water we were not greeted by the hot sun. Clouds had moved in and covered the sky. The clouds were dark and threatening.

"This sure rolled in fast," Susie said.

"We'd better head to the house. We might get wet," I laughed.

Susie rolled her eyes and sighed and said, "You are so funny. Ha ha."

Coty awoke when we popped out of the water and greeted us by licking our faces as we climbed out of the pool. We quickly put on our shoes and gathered our clothes and headed for the house. It began to rain and large heavy drops fell on our heads. The hot smell of the earth quickly vanished and was replaced by wet cooling relief. We made it back to the lake in no time. The lake looked like it was boiling as the raindrops fell on it. We quit hurrying and just enjoyed the rain as it pelted us. Parts of the path were covered by overhanging tree limbs. We stood under one of the trees and watched the lake explode with the rain.

I looked at Susie and said, "This is fun."

She nodded in agreement as the rain matted her strawberry-blonde hair to her pretty head.

When we finally reached the dam I could hear the sound of the heavy rain hitting the tin roof of the house. I loved the sound and hadn't heard it much that summer. Mamaw was standing on the back porch waving at us. We waved back and moseyed along like it was a sunny beautiful spring day. Mamaw just shook her head and went back inside. Coty began running toward the back porch. Perhaps he wasn't enjoying it as much as we were.

As we neared the back door Mamaw opened it and laid two towels on the wringer washer and threw one on the porch for Coty. Coty quickly began rubbing his face into the towel, drying himself. We grabbed the towels and ran, heading around the house to the front porch. I ran into a big puddle at the side of the house and it splashed water all over Susie and me.

We were laughing as we ascended the steps to the porch. Papaw was sitting in one of the rockers with Leo, lying at his feet. Coty went over close to Leo and shook all the water he could onto Leo. Leo opened one eye and low-growled at Coty and went back to sleep.

"Looks like you two are having fun."

"We are," I answered.

"The rain feels great," Susie said.

"It's a surprise and much needed," Papaw explained.

We sat on the porch and watched the rain fall and listened to the roof music in our ears. It was as soothing as anything could have been. Mamaw came out with soda pops for everyone and sat down with us for a moment. We talked and listened and spent the rest of the storm on the porch enjoying each other.

Thursday, August 18

Susie and I had decided to hike to the butterfly field today and word got out. James Ernest and Sadie asked if they could go with us. We couldn't say no, so the four of us headed on our hike at eight-thirty. Mamaw and Monie both liked the idea of four going instead of just the two of us, especially with the bears known to be in the area.

I had said, "What, it's better for four of us to be eaten instead of two?"

Well that was a stupid comment for me to say. I knew it as it spewed out of my mouth, and I couldn't catch it in time to stop it. They then debated whether anyone should be eaten, and maybe they should cancel the hike altogether. Our begging and pleading finally paid off and we were allowed to go since James Ernest was going. That really helped build my manhood confidence.

I decided that Coty should stay home and heal. James Ernest and I carried back packs with a picnic and first-aid sup-plies inside.

Mrs. Tuttle had gotten the pictures developed from the last hike and she showed them to us. She said she would have copies printed so we all could have them. She took pictures again. She also sent along some of her molasses ginger cookies that I could hardly eat the two other times she made them for us. At least she didn't send her potato waffles, although at the last minute she remarked that she regretted she hadn't made us any.

James Ernest had whispered to me, "We could have protected ourselves from the bears with them."

"Yes Ma'am, we regret it also," I politely said to Mrs. Tuttle.

"Timmy, you are so kind to say so," Mrs. Tuttle said with a beam in her eyes.

James Ernest just stared at me in disbelief.

I made sure to wear the cross necklace Susie had given me.

Susie wore blue shorts with a light yellow sleeveless pullover blouse with her hair pulled back in a ponytail. Sadie wore cut-off jean shorts and a sleeveless pink buttoned blouse tucked into her jeans. As soon as we were on the trail Sadie untucked her blouse and tied it in a knot revealing her stomach. Then she unbuttoned the top two buttons of her blouse.

We were off on our anticipated hike. We all carried canteens despite Sadie's complaints. She didn't want the canteen to wrinkle her blouse. She carried it to her side until she talked James Ernest into carrying it for her. We didn't bring our hiking sticks. The path to the butterfly field was flat and easy to walk. Thirty minutes into the hike Sadie complained that she was fatigued and needed a break. This was the same girl who wanted me to take a three-hour walk with her and besides, she was carrying *nothing!*

I told her that the cabin was just ahead and we could stop there for a bit. When we got to the cabin I began telling the girls all about the cabin and Tattoo Man. Sadie lost interest instantly and led James Ernest behind the cabin, probably to

French kiss. Susie wanted me to explain everything to her and I did. When I took her around to the back to show her where I saw the chicken bones we sure enough found James Ernest and Sadie kissing up a storm.

Sadie saw us and stopped long enough to say, "Are you two watching to get lessons, or are you just curious?"

Susie started to say something, but I grabbed her arm and turned her in the opposite direction. The weather had really cooled off since the storm, but things seemed to be heating up again by the look on Susie's face. Her face was flushed red and her freckles looked as if they were ready to jump off and pummel Sadie.

"We're going on now!"

"We'll be along in a bit," Sadie yelled back.

I put on my pack, and Susie and I headed on up the path. I could tell that Susie was still upset. I tried calming her. "They can kiss if they want to."

"I wouldn't care if she kissed until her mouth fell off, but she doesn't have to rub it in our noses, asking us if we needed lessons. How dare she? I have a mind to go back and knock that big mouth of hers off myself!" With that said, she turned and I had to grab her arm and lead back toward the butterflies.

"Susie, let's go on. Forget about them. Let's have fun. We wanted it to be just the two of us anyway." That seemed to calm her down a little.

She smiled and said, "You're right. Let's hurry and leave them behind."

We quickened our pace and then slowed into a nice easy walk. One in which could have lasted forever with Susie, as far as I was concerned. After ten minutes she looked over at me and reached for my hand. We walked hand-in-hand on the narrow path. The temperature was supposed to be near eighty. This morning it was cool for August, especially on the forest trail. It felt great after all the heat.

Squirrels scampered along the ground and chased each other up into the top branches of the trees. They leapt from tree to tree as they played.

"I'd like to be able to do that."

"It does look like fun. Until a hawk or a coyote catches you," Susie said.

"A bear could get us. There's always some danger no matter what you are."

"You could have gone all day without mentioning the bears. Do you think we'll see them? I bet the cubs were real cute."

"The cubs were, but the mother wasn't. She was frightening. I don't think we'll see them."

"I'd still like to see them," Susie determined.

We stopped after forty-five minutes and took drinks from our canteens and rested for a few minutes.

"It shouldn't be much farther. I hope you like it." I placed my backpack on, and we began walking again. This time I reached for her hand. She smiled at me. It had turned into a perfect morning.

We talked about the wedding coming up and how obsessed the women were over it. We talked about Clayton and his crops surviving. We talked about Coty and how he was healing. Time flew by. Soon we walked into the clearing of the butterfly field.

"This has to be it. Is this it?" Susie's face lit up as she scanned the field filled with wildflowers and busy activity. Susie led me out into the flowers. We stood among them and watched each colorful butterfly flit from one flower to another. Among the butterflies were dragonflies and damselflies flitting about the field. Birds circled overhead and all around us. Susie began naming the different flowers that she knew. I had no idea what any of them were called. I knew I had seen some of them along roads and in a few gardens. But here they were mixed together like someone had arranged an acre-sized vase.

"Timmy, this is beautiful. Thank you for bringing me to see this." She threw her arms around my neck and hugged me with all her might. I thought I had died and gone to heaven. I was standing in the most beautiful place with Susie hugging the daylights out of me. How truly wonderful those few moments were. I would never forget them. She grabbed my hand and we carefully walked through the field toward the spot where the Wolf Pack had seen the deer.

Susie asked me to be careful and not step on the flowers, which was hard since they were everywhere. I mentioned that we had seen deer in the area we were headed toward, and I told her about the hawk and where it had landed and ate the bird.

"Timmy, you know what this makes me think of?"

"How pretty this is?"

"Yes, but also how God created each one of these flowers and the different colored butterflies and birds. Isn't it amazing?"

"I guess so."

Susie continued, "God also made the moon and the stars and the black bears and coyotes and squirrels. But God also took time to create these small flowers for us to enjoy. Each petal is perfect. Each bird has its own flight. I think God wanted us to know how wonderful and great He is by creating all of this for us to see."

I had never really thought a lot about God creating each thing around me. It made sense when Susie talked so excitedly about it. I loved to listen to Susie talk. She could have told me how wonderful Thelma and Delma were, and I would have believed it in that instant. I knew she was right though, about how great God is. I just didn't know why God cared about us, especially me.

"You're right, God is great."

Susie threw her arms around me again and hugged me and then I heard the voice. "If you're going to hug him like that, you oughta kiss him also!"

Susie dropped her arms from around me and we turned to see that Sadie and James Ernest had finally arrived at the field. Susie's smile turned upside down instantly and she started to say something. I quickly said, "It's not worth it, Susie."

She slowly calmed down and said, "You're probably right. But I ain't putting up with much more."

I knew she was plenty upset when she used the word *ain't*. Susie always used correct English. Monie had always insisted that her daughters talk correctly. I heard Monie once tell Mamaw that her girls were not going to sound like "country bumpkins" and they didn't.

I yelled out, "Glad you two could join us. What do you think of it, Sadie?"

We walked back toward them as they walked toward us. Sadie answered, "It's awfully buggy, but the flowers are beautiful."

Susie whispered, "Its only buggy because she arrived." I almost laughed out loud.

"How about we have our picnic?" I suggested.

"I agree. I'm hungry," James Ernest said with that deep-throated voice of his. Sometimes when he spoke it still surprised me, especially in that deep tone.

"I saw a large rock over there we could eat on." I pointed to the southeast corner of the field where a large gray rock jutted out of the forest floor. The rock came up out the ground a couple of feet and had a top that was big enough for us to spread the picnic out and for all four of us to sit and eat. We would be able to look out over the field of flowers as we ate.

Mamaw had fixed peanut butter and jelly sandwiches for each of us and sent snack cakes. Monie had sent pickles and homemade apple sauce, and of course we had Mrs. Tuttle's molasses-ginger cookies. We drank the water from our canteens to wash it down.

Blue Jays began landing in the trees near us. James Ernest placed a piece of bread on the ledge, and we sat still. The Blue Jay looked all around and you could tell he was thinking about it and then he flew down to the rock, landed and scooped up the bread and flew off. Sadie then laid out a piece and soon another Blue Jay took it. Within minutes Blue Jays surrounded us in the trees looking for handouts.

"Let's each put a piece closer to us and see how close they'll come," I suggested.

Within a minute they were landing within a foot of us, snapping up the bits and flying off.

"Let's hold the bread in our hands and see if they'll come," Susie said.

"No way, I'm not doing that. They'll peck me," Sadie complained.

James Ernest and I thought it was a great idea, and the

three of us held our hands close to the rock with bits of snack cakes in them. The Jays would land and walk around looking at us and then at the treasures. Suddenly one got brave enough to take a bite from Susie's hand and flew away. Susie's smile returned and for the next thirty minutes we fed the Blue Jays from our hands until we ran out of food for them. One even landed on Susie's finger to get the food. Sadie then unsophisticated herself long enough to join the fun. Then she bragged about how brave she was to do it. We offered the molasses-ginger cookies to the birds. The Jays weren't about going to be tricked into it and they totally rejected them, as we had also.

As we quietly sat there the deer returned to the same spot we had seen them before. They were less than a hundred feet away and we watched them until they got spooked and left. We figured it was time to leave also. Susie and I slowly sauntered back home.

I thought, as we walked, how perfect the morning had been. We held hands as we walked.

25 THE WEDDING

I was eating breakfast by myself. Papaw had eaten and went to Robert's farm to help set up something for the wedding reception. Mamaw was watching the store, getting bait for fishermen and checking on me. I wasn't very hungry. I piddled with my eggs and bacon. I made a face with my eggs. I gave bites of my food to Coty who was sitting at attention next to my chair.

I began thinking about the summer and how quickly it had gone by. I thought about the fun I had with the Wolf Pack. Forever the pack! I thought about the day I stuck my hand in the hole at the cliff and found Coty. I thought about the midnight meetings at the cabin. We had another one last night since I was leaving that weekend to go home. We talked about all the things we had done.

We reminisced about the Wiffleball games and the hike. We talked about the bears, the waterfall, the butterfly field, the steel trap, and the ghosts. Last week, Papaw took us up to the graveyard. We cut and pulled weeds and mowed the grass. The tombstones looked so much better. Papaw thanked each of us personally with a handshake. I was real proud of our group of four. Purty had even gone with us and helped a little, while making sure he didn't pull poison ivy. Good guy.

We talked about the coonskin cap that Purty had on. James

Ernest had helped him tan it, cut it, and sewed it into a cap that fit perfectly on his head with the big tail hanging in the back. We made fun of Purty again about the poison ivy, Big Butt Rock and how he was kissing it.

I thought about my time with Susie. How she had gotten mad at me numerous times during the summer. I remembered the dead flowers I gave her and how they somehow worked. I thought about the hugs in the butterfly field and how perfect the moment was. I wondered if that's what love felt like. I hoped so.

My thoughts skipped to Uncle Morton and his broken toe and loss of hearing. I thought of Geraldine and the turkey baster. I sat at the table and laughed when I thought about James Ernest throwing pebbles at Uncle Morton while he slept in my bed and the look on James Ernest's face as he told me about it.

I thought about how I would miss Pastor White and his sermons and the Wednesday kid's nights. I understood better about God's love because of Pastor White and his love for others. I remembered the big fight that first Wednesday night. Thinking of Pastor White made me think of Miss Rebecca and Bobby Lee and how much I enjoyed spending time with them.

I had decided to leave Coty with Mamaw and Papaw. It came down to the fact that this was his home and he had plenty to do here. He enjoyed going to the lake and pestering all the fishermen and they enjoyed him being there. Coty liked watching the catfish flop on the ground after a catch. He enjoyed running the trails and playing in the creeks. Leo had even grown fond of him. I was truly going to miss him.

I was going home with my Aunt Helen who was coming

to the wedding. Her son, King, was coming with her. It would be fun riding back with them. Mom and Dad weren't able to come.

I gave Coty the rest of my food and walked into the store. "I'm going to do my chores. Do you need me to get spring water or anything else?"

"Yes. I think we could use some spring water."

"What time are we leaving?"

"Homer and Ruby will pick us up a little after one this afternoon. The wedding begins at two sharp." Papaw would not be able to go to the wedding. With the weather break, fishermen were lining the banks of the lake and Papaw said it was a good day to make some money. Besides, I don't think weddings were his cup of tea.

I walked outside with Coty right beside me. We walked up to the lake and began circling it to pick up garbage. I greeted each of the fishermen as I went. They all bent to pet Coty. When we finished I walked to the back porch and picked up the bucket. We headed for the spring. When we neared the turn-off an old rusted out pickup truck drove by pulling a flatbed trailer filled with old furniture and home goods. I stared at it in amazement. The furniture looked like things most people would throw away at a dump.

The bed of the pickup was filled also. It was partially covered with an old tarp and a young girl around my age stood next to the cab. Two smaller kids were sitting on the tarp. The cab had a man and wife in it. A small child sat in the lap of the mother. They were different looking than all the other farmers in the community. They were Negroes. I had never seen black people in Morgan County.

But where were they going? Going north on Morgan Road only went to the stone quarry. There was no outlet. There was an old beaten down house that still stood around a mile from the store. It had been abandoned years ago. Could they possibly be moving into that house? The two kids on the tarp waved back at me and smiled. The man and wife ignored my wave.

I filled the water pail and Coty and I walked back to the store. I asked Mamaw if she knew about the family. She didn't. I watched for the next hour or more for the truck to return as I helped in the store. It was busy today. Papaw returned around eleven, and I told him about the Negro family. He didn't know anything either.

"I don't think there's been a colored family in the county. I don't think there's electricity or even windows left in that house. I'm sure they couldn't be moving to that old place."

"They never have returned. I've been watching."

"We'll find out soon enough, I guess."

Mamaw went to start getting ready for the wedding. She had made a new dress last week and she told me I needed to start getting ready also.

"What do I need to do? All I need to do is change my clothes. It will take two minutes."

"Wash your ears," she yelled from her bedroom.

"Okay!" I washed my ears and changed into the new shirt and pants that Mamaw picked out in town. She bought a tie for me to wear. I even combed by hair. I put back on my same old brown scuffed leather shoes and at twenty after eleven I was ready. I sat on the front porch with Leo and Coty and watched the few vehicles that went by and a hawk that circled in the sky.

"Coty, buddy, I have to go away for awhile. I'll miss you."
My eyes began to water up. He sat next to me and looked up
into my teary eyes. "You'll be happy here with Mamaw and
Papaw. I-I-always am. Take care of them. I love you, Coty." I
pulled him to my body and hugged him. He thought I wanted
to wrestle and soon we were.

"Timmy, what are you doing? You're getting those clothes
filthy five minutes after you put them on. Dust yourself off and
get in here."

"Mamaw, I knew it was too early to put them on," I
reasoned.

"So you're blaming me for you getting them messed up."

"Yeah, something like that."

"Martin. Talk to him and watch him," Mamaw told Papaw
as she walked through the store and back into her bedroom.

"Now you've got her upset at both of us."

"Sorry," I said.

We began talking about fishing and the Negro family.
A fisherman came in for a pop and snack and a dozen night
crawlers. I went to the back porch fridge for the crawlers. James
Ernest walked into the store around twelve-thirty and asked if
he could ride to the wedding with us. I almost didn't recognize
him. He was all cleaned up with nice clothes on, and he also
had on a tie.

We went into the living room and turned on the radio and
listened to music and talked about the secret meeting we had
the night before. We discussed the summer and all we had done.
Before we closed the last meeting of the summer Randy suggested we each say what our favorite moment with the club was
and also what one thing we learned—if anything.

James Ernest went first and said he most enjoyed the night around the camp fire watching our eyes as he told the ghost story. He said he learned not to judge people too soon. He went on to explain that he wasn't sure about Randy when they first met, but now they were great friends.

"Hey, I was a jerk when I first met you guys. I'm sorry."

"You're a great guy," James Ernest told him.

Randy went next and said he had learned what friendship meant, and that he now knew he didn't have to act tough to have friends. His one moment was when Papaw shook his hand and thanked him for his work on the graveyard.

"It made me feel real good."

Purty went next and said that his favorite thing was finding Big Butt Rock. He said he had learned that walking around naked may not be so cool. He said he had decided to only do it when skinny dipping with just guys. He said he also learned just what good friends would do for a friend. "Spreading Jewelweed on my butt was a sign of true friendship."

James Ernest, "You better believe it, buddy."

Randy jumped in, "Friendship must be stronger than blood, because I wouldn't have done it." We all laughed.

It was my turn. It was hard for me, because I loved it all except for when Coty got trapped. I thought of so many things and decided on the butterfly field.

"It was like all of nature was in that one field at that moment. Like God was showing us the Garden of Eden, or what Heaven might be like. I loved it." Each of the guys shook their heads in agreement. "I learned two things. I learned what true friends will do for each other when you guys helped save Coty's life, and I learned that we have bears in the county."

We asked Coty and he howled his answer. We closed the meeting with our chant and screamed, "Forever the Pack," and sadly went home. Sad because the summer was over, but happy for the times we had.

James Ernest and I rehashed all about the meeting before Papaw appeared and said it was time to go. Homer and Ruby were in the parking lot waiting.

"Come on, Mamaw!"

She came out in her new dress and shoes. Papaw whistled at her and she blushed. She commented about how nice James Ernest and I looked, and we headed for the car. Uncle Morton was in the car also. We all squeezed in and headed for the church.

"Good to see you all," Uncle Morton greeted us.

"Good to see you, again."

We were one of the first to arrive at the church. Pastor White greeted us and teased us about being so dressed up. "Saved your Sunday best for a wedding, huh? You guys look great. You two might be able to catch you a girl to marry looking like that."

James Ernest looked at Pastor White and said, "You look pretty good yourself. Are you trying to impress someone in particular yourself?" He had on a dark suit with a snappy looking tie.

Pastor White just grinned and said, "You never know."

I couldn't believe James Ernest said that to the pastor. Who was this guy who twelve months ago wouldn't speak a word, and now here he was teasing the pastor about his love life with Miss Rebecca. I loved it. The front door of the church had white carnations with greenery on it. When I entered the church I saw white carnations on the end of each pew and large containers of white carnations, greenery, and ribbons up front on the stage. The windows were opened and a nice breeze blew in, keeping the church cooled. White carnations decorated each window. Everything was perfect.

Perfect was the word when I saw Susie sitting up front in a beautiful new white dress with a white ribbon in her hair. Brenda was beside her. She turned and saw me and motioned for me to come sat beside her. James Ernest also sat with us. She explained that Thelma and Delma were the flower girls and she and Brenda were sitting by themselves.

I told Susie and Brenda what James Ernest had said to the pastor. We all laughed.

"You look handsome," Susie told me.

"Thank you. You look *so* beautiful."

Her smiled widen and she thanked me. "I can't believe you're leaving tomorrow. I'll miss you, Timmy."

"Hey, can we sit with you guys?" I looked up to see Randy, Purty, Sadie, and Francis.

"There's room," Susie invited them to join us. Sadie sat down beside James Ernest and Randy went around to the other end of the pew and settled in next to Brenda. I saw Brenda smile. Purty and Francis filled in the rest of the pew.

Mamaw walked by and saw us all together and said, "You kids make sure you behave yourselves during the ceremony."

Purty, sitting on the end, looked up and said, "We will Mrs. Collins. You don't have to worry about us."

Mamaw looked down at him with a worried look on her face and said to Purty, "Make sure you keep your clothes on." The whole pew erupted in laughter. Mamaw walked away in a hurry, and Purty shot a look at me as I looked away.

The church was now filling up fast and the wedding would soon begin. A young man that was a friend of Dana came to the front and started playing a song on the violin signaling that everyone needed to be seated so the ceremony could begin. As the violin played softly I heard women already begin to cry. Pastor White led Dana and the best man to their places on stage. The best man was Dana's best friend through school. Susie said his name was Trent. The next to come were Idell's mom and dad down the aisle to their reserved seats in front. Next went Robert and Janice down the aisle, sitting across from the other parents. I didn't understand why they didn't sit together. There was plenty of room. I thought maybe they didn't like each other.

Next to slowly amble down the aisle were Delma and Thelma in bright green shiny new dresses. They were eating up the moment. They were carefully dropping flower petals on the floor as they meandered down the aisle. A turtle could have travel the distance faster, but they wanted to draw out their part in the wedding. Their heads moved from side to side catching everyone's admiration as they went.

When they got to our pew, Thelma looked my way, and I stuck my tongue out at her. Her eyes widened as if she was going to say something, but she kept her cool and continued her petal dropping. As they finally got to the front, Bobby Lee, the ring bearer, started down the aisle. He made up for the twins by making it to the front in record time. He waved when he saw me. I waved back.

When Bobby Lee got to the front he turned around and loudly asked me, "Where's Coty?" Everyone laughed and I put my finger to my mouth signaling for him to be quiet. Trent put his hand on his shoulder and whispered to him.

Following Bobby Lee was the maid of honor, Tammy. She wore a light-colored green dress. She was real pretty. The violinist switched songs and everyone stood and looked toward the back to see beautiful Idell begin her walk down the flower-filled aisle. Her dress was pure white with carnations on her wrist and in her hair. Everyone *oohed* and *aahed* as she walked toward the stage. Women sobbed. Susie held my hand as Pastor White welcomed everyone and opened in prayer. I noticed that Brenda was also holding Randy's hand as we sat back down.

As they went through their vows and promises to each other and Pastor White spoke, I couldn't help but think that Susie and I would replace Dana and Idell maybe eight years from now. Dana and Idell pledged their love to one another and exchanged rings. They kissed and Pastor White introduced them as husband and wife. They ran through the church to applause and laughter and folks throwing rice on them. I stood there outside the church and watched as they piled into the backseat of a car and Trent drove them away to the reception.

Our whole pew full of kids jumped into the back of Clayton's pickup. We laughed and joked all the way to the reception. The twins rode with Miss Rebecca so they wouldn't mess up their dresses.

The reception was a blast. All the food you ever imagined. Dana's friends brought guitars, a banjo, and fiddles, and played music all through the day and evening. Uncle Morton joined in playing the banjo some and singing. Folks were laughing and joking and playing games. Idell shoved a piece of wedding cake into Dana's face. He was nice and didn't get even.

I heard Bobby Lee scream, "Coty." I looked around to see Coty running into Bobby Lee's arms. Coty had come all the way up the trail and across the field to join the party. Papaw even left the store unattended for a couple of hours to join the festivities and then went back to the store. People clogged to the bluegrass that the guys were playing. They then played some rock 'n' roll that the younger generation danced to. Dana sung an Elvis Presley love song to Idell. He was really very good. The women cried again.

Idell and Dana opened their gifts for those who wanted to watch. Idell cried when she saw the quilt that the women had quilted for them. I bought them a turkey baster for my gift to them. I figured it had multiple uses.

The party went late into the night. It was the most fun event I had ever attended. I teased the twins every chance I got. When they looked at me I would start mocking the way they walked down the aisle and then stick my tongue out at them again.

"You are so rude," Delma said. "We were perfect."

"You are very rude," Thelma echoed. "Yes, we were perfect."

"The rudest," Delma worsened.

"The most rudest," Thelma added.

Some things never changed, which was a good thing, I thought.

The evening came to an end. I wanted it to go on and on. I told Susie I would see her at church in the morning, and then I would be leaving in the afternoon. At least we had one more day to see each other. I waved goodbye as they drove away. Papaw had come back up to the party after it had gotten dark. He had closed the store.

We made our way to the truck and carefully drove down the

two curves and on to the house. Coty sat on my lap. It had been a wonderful day.

26　WHAT?

The phone rang as we entered the house. "Must be Janice," Mamaw said. I went into the bedroom to take off my clothes and put on a pair of shorts. I heard Mamaw say, "What?"

I wasn't at all sleepy due to all the excitement. I changed my clothes and was pulling out a comic book to read when Papaw called my name, "Tim, come out here."

I walked into the living room where Papaw sat hugging Mamaw as she cried. I wondered what could possibly be wrong. The day was so perfect. Maybe she was still crying over the wedding. I sat in the chair and asked, "What's wrong?"

Papaw swallowed hard and tearfully said, "Tim, this evening your father died…"

"Zip-a-dee-doo-dah"

Zip-a-dee-doo-dah, zip-a-dee-ay
My, oh my what a wonderful day!
Plenty of sunshine heading my way
Zip-a-dee-doo-dah, zip-a-dee-ay
Mister Bluebird on my shoulder
It's the truth, it's actch'll
Ev'rything is satisfactch'll
Zip-a-dee-doo-dah, zip-a-dee-ay
Wonderful feeling, wonderful day!

Cherry Dumplings Recipe

2 pints of cherries (fresh is the best, or fresh frozen)

3 cups of water

3 ½ cups of sugar

2 cups of flour

1 ¼ cups of Buttermilk

Mix cherries and water with sugar–Cook

Until boiling & cherries are done

Mix flour and buttermilk - should be really thick.

Drop by teaspoonful into boiling liquid.

Reduce heat and cook about 15 minutes.

Prepare your taste buds for the best treat ever.

If they don't come out right–blame Susie.

Dear Reader,

Thank you for reading *Coty and the Wolf Pack*. I hope you enjoyed it.

The third book in the series is complete and will be out before you know it.

I've also written a romantic comedy entitled *Sleepy Valley*. It will be released very soon.

Please visit my website: www.timcallahan.net for information.

You can email me at: timcal21@yahoo.com with questions and comments.

I love hearing from readers—especially if you like the books.

May God Bless and happy reading.

Tim Callahan